CW00410299

**Merryn Allingham** was
spent her childhood mov
Unsurprisingly it gave her itchy feet, and in her twenties she
escaped an unloved secretarial career to work as cabin crew
and see the world. The arrival of marriage, children and cats
meant a more settled life in the south of England, where she's
lived ever since. It also gave her the opportunity to go back to
'school' and eventually teach at university.

Merryn has always loved books that bring the past to life, so
when she began writing herself the novels had to be historical.
She finds the nineteenth and early twentieth centuries
fascinating to research and has written extensively on these
periods in the Daisy's War trilogy and the Summerhayes
novels. She has also written two timeslip/parallel narratives
which move between the modern day and the mid-Victorian
era, *House of Lies* and its companion volume, *House of Glass*.

The Tremayne Mysteries series is a new departure into
crime but still historical (the 1950s) and still very much
focussed on people and their relationships.

For more information on Merryn and her books visit
http://www.merrynallingham.com

You'll find regular news and updates on Merryn's
Facebook page:
https://www.facebook.com/MerrynWrites
and you can keep in touch with her on Twitter:
@MerrynWrites

## Other Books in this Series

# THE DANGEROUS PROMISE

# Merryn Allingham

# THE DANGEROUS PROMISE

This novel is entirely a work of fiction. The names, characters and incidents portrayed in it are the work of the author's imagination. Any resemblance to actual persons, living or dead, events or localities is entirely coincidental.

First published in Great Britain 2020 by The Verrall Press

Cover art: Berni Stevens Book Cover Design

# Chapter One

*London, 2 June, 1953*

Nancy Nicholson arrived at Westminster Abbey as Big Ben struck seven o'clock. She had been awake since dawn, eager to bag a place as near to the cathedral entrance as possible. Disappointment, though, lay in store. The day was overcast, rows of union jacks flaring wildly in the brisk wind, but the crowd was already ten deep, waiting for a cavalcade not due for another four hours. Soldiers and policemen lined the procession route and, behind them, a continuous line of barriers kept the crowd from spilling out onto the road. She should have camped out, Nancy realised, as so many others had done, and made sure of getting a place in the first few rows. She'd be lucky to see even the roof of the Gold State Coach as it passed by, and no chance at all of glimpsing their beautiful young queen on the way to her coronation.

Excited chatter was all around and, for a while, Nancy amused herself by eavesdropping on the various conversations. It would be good, she thought wistfully, to have had a companion to share this momentous occasion, but apart from her colleagues at work, she'd found it difficult to make friends in London. In her home village of Riversley, Nancy's best friend had been Rose. Though Rose now lived in a suburb north of the city, not that far away, it was an awkward journey and, for Nancy, an expensive one. Her friend had married early and had two young children now as well as a husband to take up her time. The two of them still met occasionally, usually in Riversley when both were in Hampshire visiting family, but it was no longer the close friendship they'd previously enjoyed.

Nancy's legs had begun to ache. There was little space to sit down and the crowd had been standing for what seemed hours. Only the fortunate few at the very front, who'd come equipped with fold-up chairs as well as tents, had that luxury. Ominously, it had begun to spot with rain and here and there she noticed a black umbrella raised in anticipation. She'd forget the threat of rain and distract herself by reading. She'd brought a couple of magazines, art journals that she scanned but never seemed to have time to finish. Abingers, the auction house where she worked, was perennially short-staffed and her hours there were full. Some days she barely had time to visit the cafeteria for a drink, let alone lunch. And in the evening, after she'd trudged back to the Paddington bedsit she called home and made a rudimentary meal, she lacked the energy to do more than curl up in bed and sleep.

Opening her copy of the *British Art Journal*, her eye was caught by an article assessing the legacy left by the Festival of Britain. She was halfway down the first page when a surge from behind caused a figure to slam into her back—over the last few hours the crowd had grown hugely—and send the magazine flying.

A man bent down and rescued the journal from being trampled underfoot. 'So sorry,' he said, raising his hat. 'I was pushed…'

'It wasn't your fault. But thank you.' Nancy took the magazine back and smiled into a pair of pale grey eyes.

'Have you been here long?' he asked. 'I must admit I thought I'd have a better view than this.' He shuffled forward a few paces.

'Since seven o'clock. But there were already crowds when I got here.'

'I should introduce myself since it looks as if we might be standing side by side for some time yet. Philip March.' He held out his hand and she took it.

'It's good to meet you, Mr March.'

'Philip, please. And you?'

'Nancy. Nancy Nicholson.' She stammered a little. She'd had time now to see the man clearly. He had an attractive face, fresh complexioned with soft brown hair. And those eyes. Nancy's own eyes were grey but a quite different shade. For a moment she was fascinated and found herself staring. Then she recovered her composure and smiled again.

'You're interested in art?' he asked, pointing to the journals she was holding.

'I work in an auction house. I'm supposed to keep up with what's going on in the art world, but to be honest I'm always scrabbling for time.'

'That's interesting. Working in an auction house, I mean. I wrote an article on them a few months ago. I'm a journalist,' he explained. 'What firm do you work for?'

'Abingers. Do you know it?'

'It was one of the businesses I mentioned. I visited one morning and had a long conversation with your managing director, though I'd have liked to talk to the workers. He didn't seem too keen on my visiting the shop floor though.'

'He wouldn't be,' she said ruefully. 'Abingers has a façade it wants to maintain—genteel and effortless. You're not supposed to see the wheels!'

'Indeed, but it would have been fascinating to get behind

the façade. I wish I'd met you before, Nancy. Damn, here comes the rain.' The occasional spot was turning into a light drizzle and he reached down to open his umbrella, holding it aloft to shelter them both.

Nancy felt a small thrill of excitement. It was rare to speak at any length with a man she didn't know, and particularly an attractive one like Philip March. And he was very easy to talk to. Emboldened, she asked, 'If you're a journalist, why are you standing here? Shouldn't you have a pass for the Abbey?'

He grinned. 'No such luck. Some lucky blighter on my paper is keeping warm in there.' He gestured towards the soaring grey stone of the Abbey. 'But I'm not a royal correspondent. Nothing like it. Art, theatre, books, that's my remit. And since our royal family prefer hunting and shooting to any of those, there was little chance of my getting a ticket. I could have watched it at work—my paper's recently acquired a television and I'm sure my colleagues will be gathered round it—but I thought I'd take a few hours off to come in person. It's an amazing occasion and I wanted to witness it for myself. There may not be another coronation in my lifetime.'

'I suppose not.' Nancy was thoughtful. 'The queen *is* very young.'

'Too young. Imagine having to wear the crown at twenty-five. And being a mother to two young children as well.'

A ripple of anticipation ran through the crowd. The people at the front stumbled to their feet, in a hurry to pack away their chairs.

'Something's happening.' Nancy craned her neck. 'Can you see?' Philip March was a good head taller.

'There's a lot of bobbing of heads. I can see huge columns of servicemen—and women—on the march. Soldiers, sailors, airmen. Marching bands, too, in all their finery.' In the distance, the sound of stirring music drifted towards them.

'It's going to take a long while for the procession to pass us.'

By bending low and peering through gaps in the crowd, Nancy managed to catch fleeting glimpses of the marchers. There was always something new to see and hear. Amid the sound of tramping boots came the thunder of a hundred horses' hooves, the cavalry regiments a flash of steel and gold, their horses gleaming beneath what was now heavy rain. Then the splash of the guardsmen's red, brightened a thoroughly miserable day.

On and on it went until, at last, a line of saloons drove slowly past and behind them the carriages everyone had been waiting for, trundling towards the Abbey entrance, a glorious mix of gold and flashing jewels. For Nancy, though, they remained a blur.

'I should hoist you up,' Philip joked. 'I can just about see the Queen's velvet train, as she's walking into the cathedral. But there are far too many gaudy churchmen in the way to get a good view. Perhaps it would have been better to have seen it on television, after all.'

'I read there's going to be a film.' Nancy gave a sigh. Despite the sheltering umbrella, she was thoroughly wet and aching badly from her cramped position. 'The Odeon will be certain to show it. I'll have to wait for that.'

Philip looked down at her, bending his head beneath the umbrella. 'How about a cup of tea? I can't imagine we'll see anything more if we stick around until the ceremony is over. There's a Lyons not too far away.'

'That sounds a very good idea,' she said gratefully.

An invitation to tea from an attractive young man was a novelty. Nancy wasn't sure what her mother would say to this casual acquaintance, but Ruth Nicholson wasn't here. And wasn't she forever trying to pair Nancy off with any man under thirty she could find? At twenty-six and unmarried, she remained a sore disappointment to her parents. Perhaps tea with Philip March would balance the scales a little.

At the café, she discovered she was enormously hungry. It was nearly midday and she had eaten nothing more than a single piece of dry bread before she left the house.

'The teacakes are very good,' Philip encouraged her. 'Do have one.'

Their buttery warmth was enticing, and she didn't hesitate. 'Which paper do you work for?' she asked, wiping her hands on a paper napkin and feeling a good deal better.

'*The Daily Enquirer*. Do you read it?'

It was a prestigious broadsheet and she was impressed. There was a small part of her, though, that couldn't help wondering why such an evidently attractive and successful man as Philip March, would choose to befriend her.

Then he smiled, his eyes warm, and she thought that maybe he found her attractive, too. It gave her the confidence to say, 'I'm afraid I don't keep up with the news.'

'Too busy at that auction house, I suppose,' he said sympathetically. 'What do you actually do there?'

'I'm a second assistant in the Fine Art Department.'

It sounded so unimpressive that Nancy's confidence rapidly deflated. It had taken her eight years to climb the ladder as far as she had, and in the last year or so she'd realised that it was unlikely she would progress any further. Fine Art, it turned out, was the preserve of men, of public school, and of Oxbridge. If she'd be prepared to change departments, it was whispered, try her luck in Books, she might be more successful. But she wasn't. She loved painting.

'And what does being a second assistant entail?' He appeared genuinely interested.

'I record full details of all the items that come into the department for sale,' she said. She took a sip of her tea.

'Compile catalogues and check them when they come back from the printers, book art restorers, help in the sales room. Every day is different.'

'You sound as though you enjoy it.' Philip refilled their cups. 'That's a bonus, you know. Not many people enjoy their work. So, what's your background?'

Nancy flushed slightly. She had no doubt that the man sitting opposite her was as well-educated as those in the upper echelons of Abingers, whereas she'd managed only a school-leaving certificate and a diploma at art college.

'Quite basic.' She gave a tight little smile. 'I went to art school thinking I could make a living as an artist, but soon realised that others had ten times the talent I'd ever have. A job in the art world seemed the best alternative and I found one at Abingers.'

'And the change suited you?'

'Yes. I'm happy enough, though I'd like to do more.' She said it carefully. She itched to do more. Thought herself capable of so much more, but it didn't do to make your dreams too public. Philip March might well have contacts at the auction house, and she could be seen as a malcontent, undeserving of any promotion that might still be in the offing.

When Philip had paid their bill, they wandered out into the street. Thankfully the rain had stopped, though the sky was still a gunmetal grey.

'May I escort you home, Nancy?' he asked.

There was something endearingly old-fashioned about him, she thought, an innate courtesy. Being a gentleman, her mother would have called it. But Nancy had no wish to be walked home. With scarce funds she had made her bedsitter as homely as she could, but whatever gloss she might put on it, her accommodation was humble in the extreme. She would feel exposed if a stranger, even a delightful stranger such as

Mr March, saw where she lived.

'Thank you, but there's no need.' She smiled brightly up at him. 'I don't live far, and I imagine your paper will be wondering where you've got to.'

'It's a pity I won't have more to report back to them. In fact, they're likely to know a great deal more than I do. But your idea of seeing a film of the Coronation is excellent. It should be on release by next week. What do you think about seeing it?'

Was he asking her out? Nancy wasn't sure. 'I'd like to see it,' she said in what she hoped was a noncommittal voice.

'Good. Let me take you then. I'll leave a message at Abingers for you once I know when it's on. Are there any evenings you're not free?'

There weren't, she reflected sadly. All her evenings were much the same. A modest meal and, if she weren't too tired, an hour or two listening to the radio. Occasionally a telephone call from her mother, taken in the hall on the shared phone, with her landlady, Mrs Minns, listening in.

'Not that I can think of.'

'I'll be in touch then.' He raised his hat to her and turned to walk away.

Nancy walked slowly to the nearest trolley bus stop, a trifle dazed at the way the morning had turned out. She was still unsure how good an idea it was to meet a man in this casual fashion. Her mother plotted and planned these things for weeks. Every time she returned home, something had been 'arranged'. Some poor, unsuspecting man had been dragooned to escort her to the local theatre, or the summer fair, or partner her at one of the endless dinner parties that seemed fashionable among the few friends the Nicholsons had.

But today, it seemed, Nancy had arranged her own date.

She was due to visit Riversley this weekend. Should she mention the man she'd just met? Perhaps not. A teacake and a cup of tea at Lyons Corner House was hardly a date and Philip might never leave the message he'd promised.

# *Chapter Two*

Two days later a note appeared in Nancy's pigeonhole. The receptionist, who'd taken the message, was agog with interest.

'Have you got yourself a bloke then?' Brenda Layton asked. 'If so, it's about time.'

Nancy gave her a tight little smile but tucked the note away in her handbag to read at her desk. Philip was suggesting they meet the following week, a Wednesday evening, at the Leicester Square Odeon. He'd be in the foyer from seven and hoped she could make it. If not, could she telephone his newspaper and leave him a message? A telephone number for *The Daily Enquirer* was written at the bottom of the note, and *Only to be used in emergencies* written beneath the number.

She was exhilarated, hardly believing that Philip March had kept his promise. Every so often, when she was alone, she retrieved the invitation from her handbag and re-read it. Next Wednesday! The intervening days would seem long and first she had to face a visit home.

*

Her mother's sole topic of conversation that weekend was the forthcoming village fair and how she was to manage two stalls at the same time. It was tedious, but it spared Nancy any new suitor her mother had managed to secure since she was last at home.

'I always run the cake stall, don't I?' Ruth Nicholson complained. 'But now Mavis Threadgold has decided to go on a trip to France—France, I ask you—and I've been asked to double up and help with the book stall as well.'

Nancy managed a sympathetic murmur at the first few mentions, but when on Sunday morning, her mother said, 'Books are your kind of thing, Nancy. Books and pictures. You could do the stall,' she decided it was time to leave for London, a little earlier than she'd planned.

'Make sure you make a note of the date. I shall need help,' were her mother's parting words at Riversley station.

Nancy gave a vague nod. It was still early June and autumn was weeks away. Meanwhile a far more attractive date was drawing close. She'd contemplated whether or not to mention Philip March to her parents—there was a bubble of pride pushing her to confide—but her mother's constant complaints and her father's desire to spend every day in his allotment meant the right opportunity never seemed to emerge. In the end, she was glad she'd kept silent. She and Philip knew virtually nothing of one another and their second meeting might prove a disaster, meaning her mother's hopes dashed and an even more frantic effort by Ruth to find a man to marry her daughter.

It had been several months since the last ghastly attempt. A nephew of one of Harry Nicholson's former work colleagues had been invited to stay. For her mother to issue an invitation to dinner was an occasion, but an overnight guest in the cramped but repressively neat bungalow, was unheard of. It was a measure of Ruth Nicholson's despair, and it had all come to nothing. Nancy and the young man had looked at each other, muttered a few awkward phrases, and inwardly shaken their heads.

*

The following Wednesday, Nancy dressed with care. Her best summer dress, a pretty floral cotton, and a cashmere cardigan her godmother had given her years before but still as good as new. She had a lot to thank her godmother for, Nancy thought, hurrying to catch the trolleybus at the end of the road. If it hadn't been for the old lady's legacy, she would never have attended art college. Her parents had been unwilling to help; they'd made that clear. If she had gone to secretarial school, learned shorthand and typing like other girls in her class, they would have found the necessary funds. But art! Certainly not.

Philip was waiting for her in the Odeon foyer, smartly dressed and carrying a rolled umbrella. He looked every bit the London businessman. He'd been wearing a suit when they'd first met, she recalled, but then he'd come straight from his office that day. Off duty, she'd supposed he would look more casual, even a little untidy. But he'd dressed for the occasion, hadn't he? Dressed for her. She was thrilled by the thought.

The Coronation on film was every bit as powerful as Nancy had imagined. Rich, regal, deeply symbolic. Tears pricked at her eyes when the young queen, holding both sceptre and orb, was crowned by the Archbishop of Canterbury, the Abbey ringing with shouts of God Save the Queen as St Edward's Crown was placed on her head. Philip sat still and quiet beside Nancy. She had no idea if the ceremony had affected him as much as it had her, but afterwards as they filed out into the brilliantly lit square, he said, 'That was worth a visit, wasn't it?'

'It was wonderful. Thank you for suggesting we go. And for booking the tickets.'

'I was happy to do it. I felt sorry for you at the Abbey—you barely saw a thing. Mind you, I saw little more. Now how about a drink to round off the evening?'

'I'd like that,' she said, though inwardly feeling nervous. She rarely visited a public house and had no idea what she should order. But when they walked into the *Lamb and Flag*, Philip strode up to the bar and ordered for them both.

'A scotch and soda and a Babycham,' he said to the man polishing glasses behind the counter.

'The lady wants a Babycham?'

'That's what I said.' She was surprised at the snappiness in Philip's voice.

'Sorry, mate. I didn't hear her ask for it.'

'She didn't.' Philip stared at the barman.

The man shrugged his shoulders. 'Comin' up, squire.'

Philip turned to smile at her. 'Why don't you take a seat, Nancy? I'll bring the drinks over.'

A young barmaid was clearing a corner table and Nancy slid onto the wooden settle.

'So, what did you do at the weekend?' Philip asked, when he'd deposited their drinks and two bags of Smith's crisps on the table. 'I hope you had a better time than me. I was forced to spend it working. Deadline looming, I'm afraid.'

Nancy took an experimental sip of her drink and found it innocuous. 'I went home. To Riversley. It's where my parents live.'

'And Riversley is…?'

'A small village in deepest Hampshire.'

'It sounds beautiful.'

'It is, but very quiet.'

'Which is why, I imagine, you moved to London.' He

raised his glass to her.

She gave a wry smile. 'It's true there aren't too many auction houses in Riversley.'

'I'd love to see the village,' he said unexpectedly. 'I love the countryside but don't get much chance to visit.'

Was he expecting her to invite him? She had a moment of panic. But then he said, 'I've really enjoyed this evening, Nancy. I wonder… would you like to have dinner one night?'

She felt a flutter of pleasure. Another date and somehow a more serious one. From a chance meeting to this evening's cinema visit and now an invitation to dinner.

'I'd like that very much.'

Nancy was already looking forward to it. He was an interesting man. As they'd walked to the *Lamb and Flag*, he'd talked about his work; it was clear Philip had travelled widely and met a number of important people. And the articles he'd written were varied—profiles on up-and-coming artists, investigations into art theft, reviews of the latest exhibitions. It was evident he was a valued member of the *Daily Enquirer's* staff. Interesting and handsome, Nancy mused and, as far as she could tell, unattached. She liked him enormously.

'Next week? Thursday perhaps?' he suggested.

'That would be fine.' She took a more confident sip of her drink.

'Then I'll collect you around seven. Where do you live?'

Nancy swallowed hard. She'd known that eventually she might have to confess where she lived and, though she knew she'd made the best of the home she had, it didn't stop her feeling ashamed that she hadn't managed to do better.

'I'm in a bedsitter,' she mumbled. 'Number sixteen Chilworth Road.'

Philip took a pocket book from the inside of his jacket and scribbled a note. He hadn't baulked at the address or the idea of a bedsitter, and Nancy breathed more easily.

Tucking his notebook away, he looked down at his watch. 'I'm afraid I have to go. I need to get back to the office—late copy to file— but I'll see you next Thursday at seven.'

He handed her the cardigan she'd slipped off and together they walked out of the pub and into the warm evening. At the corner of the street, he gave her a chaste kiss on the cheek. 'Bye, Nancy. Look after yourself,' he said.

'I will—'she began, when a trolley bus came into view and she started forward, meaning to run for it. 'I should catch that.'

'Go!' He was laughing and waved to her as she jumped onto the platform. From her vantage point, she watched his figure slowly fade into the distance and only then went to find a seat. Her heart was beating a little too fast, and not just from the sprint. She had a boyfriend! And one chosen by herself, not by her mother. To be fair, Philip had done the choosing, but wasn't that always the case? It might be the 1950s, a new Elizabethan age according to the commentators, but women must still wait to be chosen.

Philip had been worth waiting for, she reflected, looking through the dusty bus window, but hardly noticing the bright lights of the West End. He might dress a little formally, his manners might be a little old-fashioned, but he was generous and polite and very attractive.

That night, as Nancy undressed for bed, she hummed a popular tune.

# Chapter Three

'How's that chap who left you the message?' Brenda asked her, when she walked through Abingers' front entrance the next morning.

'Fine,' Nancy answered blithely.

'So, when are we going to see him?'

'I'm not sure why you'd want to, Brenda.'

'Just taking an interest,' the receptionist muttered and flounced back to her desk.

Abingers might see Philip at the annual Christmas party, Nancy thought—staff were allowed to bring a guest—but that was nearly half a year away and she daren't think that far ahead. Just to know he was part of her life now made her very happy.

'There you are.' Sidney Harker, her department head, swooped down on her as she went to climb the stairs to the third floor. 'We need you, Nancy. Professor Tremayne is here. He's authenticated a Francia and wants to be present when we hang it. You're required to check measurements.'

Taking off her hat and coat on the move, Nancy hurried to follow Mr Harker to the Tribune Room, at the same time delving into her workbag for a notebook and pen. She had never met the professor, though she'd glimpsed him occasionally being whisked into the Managing Director's office. He was an important person, she knew, and revered at Abingers for his expertise. The house often consulted him for valuations, and Nancy had heard him once on the wireless being interviewed on the market for Renaissance paintings.

A small group of people had gathered in the Tribune Room, the chief curator among them. Aubrey Simmonds came puffing up to her. 'Have you your notebook with you, Miss Nicholson?'

Two of the warehousemen were standing beside a large blanket-covered painting, looking bored, while Mr Simmonds fussed around with tape measure and long ruler and Mr Harker, Nancy's immediate boss, stood with arms folded, looking at the blank wall. He made an irritated little finger wag at her to come closer and, as she did, Professor Tremayne looked up from his notes and smiled at her.

'I don't think we've met before. Leo Tremayne.' He held out his hand.

'Nancy Nicholson,' she said, surprised. It was unusual for a visiting expert to notice anyone who wasn't a manager.

The professor turned to Mr Simmonds to gauge his opinion and, while he talked to the curator, she looked at him closely. In his forties she reckoned, slim figure, still handsome, hair silvering, deep brown eyes.

'Right, Miss Nicholson.' Turning to her, Leo Tremayne rolled off the measurements of the painting. 'Now… we're aiming for five foot six to the middle of the picture. Can you indicate?'

Nancy did the calculation and with the ruler Mr Simmonds had handed her, indicated a point on the wall.

'Let's see.' Leo Tremayne stood back looking at the empty space, then walked first to the left, then the right.

'Negative space,' he said. 'We need to get it right. The space the spectator creates when they walk from one work to another, when their eyes scroll from one to another. What do you think?'

Both the curator and Mr Harker shuffled towards the professor, considering the paintings that would hang on either side of the Francia. It mattered to them, Nancy thought. Getting it right meant more interest in the picture, higher advance bids, and greater profit for Abingers.

'What do *you* think, Miss Nicholson?'

She was aware of heavy frowns—the senior members of the team would not like her included in the conversation. She tried, though, to concentrate on the professor's question and after several minutes, said, 'I think it's right.'

Leo Tremayne nodded. 'Bill? Derek?'

'Say the word, prof,' one of the warehousemen said.

The picture was hoisted into place, the measurements checked and double-checked, and when her superiors had verified that the painting was indeed perfectly hung, the circle of men relaxed, their shoulders visibly loosened. Bill and Derek rolled up the protective blanket for further use and made a quick exit.

Mr Harker's lips formed a thin line. 'Thank you, Miss Nicholson. You may return to your work now.'

'Yes, thank you, Miss Nicholson.' Leo Tremayne said. 'A splendid job.' Nancy felt bathed in the warmth of his smile.

\*

Philip had suggested they try a restaurant in Maida Vale, a short walk from Chilworth Road. It had only recently opened and he liked the look of the menu. When they met that Thursday evening, Nancy was still bubbling with pleasure at having played a part in the picture hanging and couldn't wait to tell Philip over supper, thinking he'd be interested.

'Tremayne?' he questioned. 'I don't recognise the name.'

'I believe he's very well-known,' Nancy said uncertainly.

'Not in my part of the art world,' Philip said briskly. 'Now what shall we have? The fillet of sole looks good. And to accompany? Boiled potatoes and peas, I think. Let's make it two of those.'

Nancy had barely looked at the menu but she was sure he was right. Eating out was a novelty to her and she was willing to be guided. But Philip was wrong about Leo Tremayne. If a man was interviewed on the wireless as a Renaissance expert, if he held sway at a prestigious auction house such as Abingers, he must be more well-known than Philip acknowledged. It was strange he hadn't recognised the professor's name.

*

Over the next few months, they ate at the same restaurant several times. A flower seller began to call, hoping to find a romantic couple or two willing to spend a shilling. The first time Philip saw him, he called the man over; then, kissing her hand, presented Nancy with a single long-stemmed red rose. After that, every time they ate at the restaurant, Nancy returned home with a flower for her room.

As July passed into August and the weather grew warmer, they took picnics every weekend to one or other of the London parks. One day, they took the train out to Richmond and spread a blanket beneath a canopy of ancient trees, while in the distance a herd of red deer grazed undisturbed. They ate chicken sandwiches, followed by a delicious fruit tart, and afterwards lay full length on the long grass, the sun's rays playing hide and seek between the branches.

'I think you should live in a park,' Philip teased, winding a long strand of her hair around his finger. 'You fit so perfectly.'

He bent to kiss her on the lips. In response, she reached

up and pulled him close. 'You would have to come and live there, too,' she said.

'Who's to say I won't?'

Another kiss, his lips warm and hard against hers. She wrapped her arms more tightly around him, her lips parted. To her disappointment, Philip rolled to one side and away from her. He was too much of a gentleman to take their lovemaking further, Nancy thought, and she was too shy to initiate it. But for the first time in her life, she had someone who truly cared for her.

She knew she should write home and tell her parents about Philip, but Nancy also knew how the script would unfold. An invitation to Riversley would follow on the heels of her letter, Ruth Nicholson beside herself with excitement, intent on making elaborate plans for Philip's visit. Too elaborate. There'd be resentment, too, Ruth angry that her daughter had succeeded where she had failed. Foreseeing the embarrassment that lay ahead, Nancy stayed her hand. At some time, Philip must visit Riversley, must meet her parents, but she couldn't bear the thought of taking a pin to her balloon.

When autumn arrived and it was too cold to picnic, Philip devised a programme of talks and theatre visits. Nancy smiled to herself—it was almost as though he'd taken it on himself to educate her. She was happier, though, than she'd ever expected to be. No longer lonely. No longer feeling the odd one out. And falling more and more under Philip's spell every time she saw him. His figure walking towards her gave her a thrill, his kiss made her feel she could melt.

\*

Nancy met Rose for lunch one day just before Christmas. Rose was not on the telephone and, in any case, telephoning was impossible for Nancy, policed as it was by her landlady. Instead, she wrote letters, but had managed only one to her friend during these last blissful months.

As soon as she walked through the café door, Rose bounced to her feet and wrapped her in a huge hug.

'You look wonderful, Nancy. Positively glowing. Is it love?'

The question had been asked teasingly, but Nancy was serious when she answered. 'I think so.'

Rose stared at her. 'You're in love?'

'I must be,' she said.

Nancy had little by which to judge her feelings, but she looked forward to being with Philip. Eagerly. She enjoyed talking to him, had fun wandering the museums and galleries together, loved the meals they shared. And wanted his kisses, badly. What else did love entail?

Rose beamed across the table at her. 'So, who is he? And when can I meet him?'

'Soon,' Nancy assured her. 'He's a journalist on *The Daily Enquirer* and his hours aren't regular, but I'm sure I can organise a meeting.' It would be wonderful to introduce Philip as her boyfriend. Her long-term boyfriend, since it was five months since they'd met.

'You must come to dinner,' Rose said. 'Just choose a day.'

But when Nancy mentioned to Philip the possibility of their visiting Rose and her husband—dinner had been suggested, she told him—he prevaricated.

'Not at the moment, darling. I've too much work on.'

'Rose has offered us any day we can manage. She's happy to fit in,' Nancy pursued.

'I don't think so. I'm very busy right now.'

She found it difficult to believe. He wasn't too busy to meet her every week, sometimes twice a week. Couldn't they simply make one of those evenings a time when they visited Rose? Perhaps he was shy, unsure of meeting her friends. It seemed unlikely, but one never knew. In certain circumstances, even the most confident-seeming people could be shy.

'It would be good for me to meet your friends, too,' she said, thinking it might ease the way to dinner at Rose's.

'That's not a good idea at all.' His voice was cold.

Nancy was startled. 'Why ever not?'

'They're old newspaper hacks,' he said, in a different tone, laughing it off. He took her hand and squeezed it. 'You wouldn't enjoy their company, believe me.'

## *Chapter Four*

After Philip's reluctance to meet her friends, Nancy had been dubious about inviting him to Abingers' Christmas party, due in a few weeks' time. She'd felt sure he would refuse but, to her surprise, he was happy to agree. She was delighted. For the first time since she'd joined the firm, she would be bringing a guest. A man she could be proud of. Somehow it made her position in the auction house feel more secure. There was satisfaction, too, in confounding Brenda Layton, who over the months had been sharp in her mockery of Nancy's so-called boyfriend, evidently not believing that such a person existed.

Abingers had a tradition of serving cocktails before the party proper began, inviting their most valued experts to share a celebratory drink. As soon as Nancy walked into the room, she saw Leo Tremayne. A colleague whispered to her that the great man had engagements elsewhere that evening, but had dropped into Abingers to wish everyone a Happy Christmas.

Philip had gone to the bar to fetch their drinks when the professor came across the room and shook her hand. 'How are you Miss Nicholson?' It was gratifying he remembered her.

'I'm well, thank you, Professor.'

'And still measuring?'

'Among other things,' she said curtly. She was tired of having her work disparaged.

'Of course. Your days must be very busy.'

Nancy felt sorry for the way she'd spoken. 'Are you going away for Christmas?' she asked, hoping to make amends.

'I am. I'm off to Cornwall tomorrow.'

'It's a beautiful place for a holiday.'

Out of the corner of her eye, she saw Aubrey Simmonds, the chief curator, frowning heavily. Talking at length with the firm's elite was not party manners, it seemed, but Nancy was unrepentant.

'It's my family home, in fact. A fishing village, Port Madron. My father and brother live there, and I'll be spending Christmas with them—possibly New Year.'

'Only possibly?'

'I'm on standby to go to New York.'

What a glamorous life he must lead, she thought. '*I'm* on standby to spend it at Riversley.' She spoke tongue-in-cheek.

When his eyebrows shot up, she said, 'Riversley is *my* home village.'

Leo gave what sounded like a chuckle, but was interrupted before he could say more when Aubrey Simmonds glided across the floor and inserted himself between them, guiding the professor away.

When Nancy turned, it was to see Philip glaring at her.

'Is anything wrong?' she asked quietly.

'You seem mighty friendly with that man.'

'That's Professor Tremayne. Abingers consult him from time to time. I met him back in the summer. I told you about it—when I was asked to help hang the Francia. Do you remember? We must have done a good job. The painting fetched a fortune.'

Philip fixed her with a chilly stare. 'You need to be careful, Nancy. He looks to me a snake-in-the-grass kind of chap. A bit too obvious with the charm.'

'The charm?' she asked, startled.

'Lays it on with a trowel,' Philip muttered, and turned away from her to walk across the room to join a giggling Brenda Layton and a group of girls from the clerical department.

For the next few hours, he seemed to take pleasure in ignoring Nancy. The cafeteria had been decorated with the requisite number of balloons and cardboard Santas, and its tables arranged end to end, so that guests sat in two long rows. Nancy watched sadly as Philip walked along the line and deliberately chose the seat next to Brenda. It was as far away from her as possible.

By the time they caught the bus back to Chilworth Road, though, he seemed to have recovered his good humour, asking Nancy what she would like to do for the New Year and suggesting plans for the celebration. She was puzzled by his switch of mood, finding it disturbing. But Philip seemed not to notice, as always walking from the bus stop with her hand-in-hand and kissing her on both cheeks to say goodbye.

\*

On New Year's Day itself, they walked by the Serpentine. A weak sun shone from a sky of winter blue, but even at midday, frost still rimed the grass which crunched beneath their feet. Standing at the water's edge, Philip took both her hands in his. 'It's a new year and time for change.'

Panic gripped Nancy. Was he preparing to say goodbye? The memory of the Christmas party hung heavily between them.

'I feel it's time I met your parents, Nancy,' he announced.

She was confused, not knowing what to feel. Relief that,

far from leaving, Philip was intent on forging a more serious relationship. But dread, too. What would he think when he walked into the Nicholson's cramped bungalow for the first time? That was unimportant, she told herself. He'd had a glimpse of her poky bedsitter—all Mrs Minns would allow—without turning a hair and, for all Nancy knew, he might live in similarly humble surroundings. She didn't know; she had never been to his flat. He worked there as often as he worked at the newspaper, he told her, and the flat was too much of a mess to invite her in.

It was her mother's reaction that she most dreaded. She knew exactly how it would go. At first, Ruth would greet her visitor enthusiastically—too enthusiastically. Would Philip discern the falsity? Nancy was fairly sure he would. But more concerning was the churn below the surface. Her mother would be silently picking holes, finding fault. A mass of conflicts. Delighted that here at last was a possible husband for Nancy, but unhappy that her daughter had chosen the man for herself after Ruth's years of fruitless searching. A man the Nicholsons knew little about, a virtual stranger. That was not the way they liked to conduct their life. And when she and Philip had returned to London, Nancy would get one of those dreadful phone calls from home, standing in the bare hall while she listened to her mother asking her what on earth she was thinking, courting a man no one knew—and Ruth *would* use the word 'courting'— and a newspaper man at that. It was well-known they were drunkards, if not worse.

'Your family?' Philip prompted.

'It would be good for you to visit,' she managed to say, staring at the cold stretch of water. A duck took flight as she watched, lumbering slowly into the air. For all its awkwardness, Nancy would like to have followed.

'I have a particular reason for wanting to meet them as

soon as possible,' Philip said meaningfully.

She must have looked baffled because he teased, 'Can't you guess?'

'I'm afraid not.'

'Marriage, Nancy, marriage.' When she still looked bewildered, he frowned. 'Our marriage.'

Philip was the man she wished to spend her life with, of that Nancy was certain, but she'd never been sure of his feelings. He must like her to continue seeing her, but did he love her? He'd never told her how he felt. Actions speak louder than words, she could hear her mother saying. And since they'd met last June at the Coronation, Philip had been an assiduous escort, a trustworthy friend. He'd shared kisses with her, even a cuddle or two, but had never pressured her for more.

Nancy had known someone who had—when she first arrived in London. The man had rented the room beneath hers. She'd been very young, just eighteen, and felt both exhilarated and terrified at being part of an amazing city. She'd considered the man's advances a kind of coming-of-age and gone along with it, though the experience had been dismal. Hot, sticky embraces, a fumbling with her clothes, kisses that travelled everywhere. Their relationship, such as it was, had lasted a few months, until one day she saw him smuggling into his room a buxom brunette some years older than himself. Mrs Minns had seen the woman, too, and that had been the end of the lodger. The landlady had evicted him that night and Nancy hadn't been sorry to see him go. After that, she'd been disinclined to find anyone new. She'd wanted Philip, though, from the moment they'd first met. Philip was different.

'I want to marry you,' Philip spelled out, as though talking to a child. 'And I want to do it properly. Ask your father's permission.'

Naturally, he would. He would do everything properly. Philip was what her mother called a true gentleman.

'That's a wonderful idea.' She felt her face glow. 'Getting married, I mean.'

'You didn't think of it yourself.'

'I hadn't thought you'd want to,' she said humbly.

He bent down and kissed her full on the lips. 'I don't know why that is. I love you, Nancy. I may not be the most demonstrative of men, but you can believe me when I tell you so. And because I love you, I want to marry you. So, what do you say about my coming to spend next weekend at Riversley?'

# Chapter Five

'How do you do? I'm so pleased to meet Nancy's parents at last.' Philip March stood on the bungalow's doorstep and gave each of the Nicholsons a firm shake of the hand.

Standing back to allow the young man through the door, Nancy's father was all smiles. He had been the one to reply to his daughter's letter mentioning Philip, while her mother had kept an ominous silence. Ruth Nicholson was as annoyed as Nancy had expected. She'd had no involvement in this new relationship, yet Philip March might prove the man for whom she'd been searching. Her mother's face, Nancy saw, had been wiped clean of expression.

'I can't think why Nancy hasn't mentioned you before,' Ruth complained, leading the way into the sitting room.

'Nor me, Mrs Nicholson,' Philip responded. 'But I'm delighted to be here.' He looked around and made a play of warming his hands at the fire. 'This is such a cosy room.'

At a stretch, it could be described as 'cosy' Nancy supposed, if only for its smallness, but she'd always disliked the room, so lacking in anything resembling beauty. The same beige chairs and hessian carpet, the same bare walls and absence of ornaments.

'Please take a seat, Mr March. May I get you a cup of tea

after your journey?' Her mother sounded stilted, as though she were reciting the lines of a play.

'Philip, please. Tea would be wonderful.' He beamed at Ruth. 'How kind of you to suggest it.'

Nancy saw her mother melt slightly beneath his smile and, when Ruth reappeared with a tray of tea and biscuits, it was to say in a warmer voice, 'I hope you'll enjoy your stay with us.'

'How could I not?' Philip took the proffered cup from his hostess. 'I love the countryside. Unfortunately, I don't manage to visit very often, but when we drove from the station, I thought what a beautiful village Riversley was.'

Ruth Nicholson melted some more. 'It is beautiful. Nancy can take you on a walk tomorrow. It's a shame you don't get out of London much. Nancy told us you were a journalist— I thought journalists travelled widely.' There was a note of suspicion in Ruth's voice.

'I certainly travel for work at times,' Philip said pleasantly. 'But I tend to go to locations that aren't at all beautiful. I'm a feature writer, you see, and spend my time interviewing all kinds of characters who can live in some pretty rum places.'

'You must tell us about them,' Harry said rousingly, 'but do have a biscuit. You must be hungry and we don't eat until six. A treat coming up, though. Ruth has made one of her splendid pies. Steak and kidney.'

'My absolute favourite,' Philip said, taking a biscuit and smiling once more.

*

At supper that night, Ruth Nicholson returned to her inquisition. 'It would have been nice to have met you a while ago, Philip.' She cast an accusatory glance at her daughter. 'How long have you known each other?'

'I met Nancy on Coronation Day, would you believe? Our lovely young queen was crowned on the second of June and, on the very same day, I met the love of my life.'

Nancy blinked at the fulsomeness. But she shouldn't be surprised. Philip had got the measure of her parents immediately and was playing the role expected of him.

'Well, I must say…' Ruth's cheeks had plumped up like a guinea pig who'd eaten double his rations.

'I'm sorry if that sounds a little flowery,' Philip apologised. 'But it's how I feel. It's why I'm here. Nancy told me you never visit London and I realised that I must come to you. It was high time you met the man who loves your daughter. Nancy is a wonderful girl and I want to marry her. I'm hoping you'll like me enough to agree.'

Both her parents were looking dazed at this onslaught. 'It's really Harry that you should be asking,' Ruth said faintly.

What is this, Nancy thought angrily, the nineteenth century?

'Absolutely no need to ask, my boy.' Harry Nicholson was at his most jovial. 'Nancy is a big girl. It's up to her, but I'm impressed that you thought to do so. Not many would these days.'

Ruth jumped up to clear the supper dishes and bestowed a bright smile on her future son-in-law. 'If it suits you and suits Nancy,' she said in a trilling voice, 'who are we to stand in the way of true love?'

It was one ghastly cliché after another. Nancy's spirits, already low, sunk even further. How on earth was she to get through this weekend?

But somehow she did.

Apart from an ancient Saxon church, St Saviour's, Riversley was indistinguishable from a hundred other English villages—cottages clustered around the green, a village store, a cosy pub—but it lay in countryside made for walking, lush meadows giving way to gently wooded hills. Philip thought it beautiful and, keen to explore, the two of them spent hours walking the surrounding lanes or tramping through woods, across fields, and along the river bank. Nancy was grateful since it kept them away from the bungalow for as long as possible. If she had to hear her mother apologise once more for the tiny guest room—it *was* little more than a large cupboard—Nancy knew her nerves would shred so completely they'd disappear.

Her parents' reactions were exactly as she had predicted, her father welcoming, her mother tetchy. But Ruth was in awe of Philip, Nancy could see, despite her mother's pretence. He was a man who wrote for the papers, no less, and not one of those shabby tabloids either, but the quality press. What a thing to tell those gossiping neighbours. In the end, though, it was her sweetheart's unstinted praise of the steak and kidney pie that sealed her mother's approval. It gave Nancy a rare moment of humour.

As the weekend proceeded, she felt stifled by her parents' overwhelming pleasure. Understanding that pleasure made it no easier to bear. For years they had been waiting for her to meet the man of her dreams—my God, *she* was thinking in clichés now—and had almost given up hope. She'd been a disappointment to them from birth, and her lack of a husband was just one more vexation to add to the count.

In a rare moment of candour, her mother had once confessed to suffering multiple miscarriages before Nancy's birth. Probably after it, too, though the subject had never again been raised. By some strange quirk, Nancy had been the baby to survive, but she'd been the wrong baby. The wrong sex. She should have been a boy, that's what Harry had wanted and what Harry wanted, so did Ruth. Nancy was a girl and, even worse, a girl who did not appreciate girly things. She had no interest in parties or dressing up or, as she grew older, in finding a boyfriend.

All Nancy had ever wanted to do was draw and paint. Her entire childhood seemed to have consisted of scavenging for paper, begging pencils from other children and, when she began a Saturday job at the newsagents, using her hard-earned shillings to buy her first set of oil paints. When she'd decided she wanted to go on to art school, her parents had been scandalised. Only dropouts went to art school, they said. There was no way it would provide her with a means to earn her living before she married. It was practical skills she needed. Maybe train as a nurse? Or learn catering? Better still, go into office work. That was clean and the hours were good. In an office she was more likely to meet an up-and-coming young man. A clerk perhaps, destined to rise steadily in his career. A good husband and father.

But, for once, fortune had favoured Nancy. The year before she applied to art school, the godmother she'd rarely seen, Harry's estranged elder sister, Edith, had died unexpectedly and left her goddaughter a legacy. Despite anything the Nicholsons could say against it, Nancy had the money to pay her expenses at art school. Short of turning their daughter out of the house, they could do nothing but grit their teeth and suffer as she returned home each week with one challenging 'work' after another— in their opinion the word itself was a misnomer.

Nancy had never felt particularly welcome in her home, but during the two years she'd spent at art school her parents' resentment had been tangible and, after securing her diploma, her decision to leave home had been inevitable. She hadn't sufficient funds to continue to study for a higher diploma, but she had a school-leaving certificate and a basic qualification in art. She would try her luck in London. Once more, her parents were scandalised. To leave home at seventeen, not even eighteen, and go to a city like London to live alone, was truly shocking—everyone at chapel knew what people got up to there. The neighbours duly gossiped and the Nicholsons suffered in stoic silence. But Nancy was free at last.

London wasn't the paradise she'd hoped for, but after several dead-end jobs in a café and a corner shop, she'd seen an advertisement she thought could change her life: a vacancy for an assistant in the Fine Art department of a prestigious London auction house. Nancy would start on the lowest rung, but at least she would be on the ladder. In the end, the job hadn't changed her life entirely. But it had made it better, and now Philip was making it better still.

# Chapter Six

On Monday morning Nancy returned to work exhilarated, the engagement ring Philip had presented her on their final walk around Riversley strung on a chain around her neck. Rings, other than wedding bands, were frowned on by the auction house as a possible danger to the delicate materials they handled. In any case, Nancy wanted to keep this wonderful new secret to herself, for the moment at least. Every few minutes she found herself placing her hand against her chest to feel the ring's reassuringly solid form.

The ring wouldn't have been her choice: a large ruby, flashing brilliant red, and set in a circle of sparkling diamonds. A little too showy for her taste. But Philip had chosen it and that made it special. Despite her fears, the weekend had proved miraculous. And today the whole world felt special. She had never expected to be this happy, to have a man she loved by her side, and to know her parents were pleased. She had finally confounded their expectations.

Her morning was spent tucked away in her small office on one of the upper corridors, organising the catalogue for a forthcoming sale. Few of her colleagues walked this way and even fewer visitors, so she was surprised when a tentative knock had her look up to see Leo Tremayne in the doorway.

'Miss Nicholson, isn't it?'

'Yes, it is. Are you lost, Professor? Perhaps I can help.'

'Lost? I suppose I must be,' he said vaguely. 'I should be meeting your chief curator around now.'

'His office is on the first floor,' Nancy said. 'Can I take you there?'

'Thank you. That would be kind.'

She wondered at his being lost, since Professor Tremayne had been in and out of Abingers for years. He should have known the way to Aubrey Simmonds' office, but then a man like the professor lived in a rarefied world.

As they travelled down in the lift together, he kept the conversation going. Did she enjoy her work in the auction house? What did she enjoy most? What about picture hangings—had she done any more since he'd last seen her? Nancy was flattered by his interest, but also a little nervous. He was such an eminent man and, as she was constantly reminded, she occupied a lowly position in the firm's hierarchy.

At the chief curator's door, the professor bid her a friendly goodbye. 'I hope to see you again, Miss Nicholson, when I'm next here.'

Nancy wasn't sure she shared that hope, finding his company a trifle daunting. But he was an attractive man and extremely knowledgeable. Someone she would have liked to have learned from.

*

That evening, Philip appeared unexpectedly on the doorstep of the house in Chilworth Road. Mrs Minns tutted loudly at the sight of a man on her threshold and glared at Nancy, who had arrived in the hall a few minutes after her. The landlady's grim expression dared her to take this 'gentleman caller' up to her room.

'I'm afraid we'll have to talk here,' Nancy murmured, keenly aware of the drab walls and the single dim light bulb hanging from a dusty lampshade. But at least Mrs Minns had disappeared.

'That's okay. I won't be long. I know we're due to meet on Friday, but I couldn't wait to see you. I've been thinking about our wedding, you see. Ever since I got back from Riversley. And I want it to be in June.'

'But it's March already,' Nancy stammered. 'That's only three months away.'

'Good to see you can count.' He tussled her hair. 'I can't wait for us to be married, that's the thing. I phoned your parents this morning—so helpful they're on the telephone—and they've promised to book for a mid-June wedding. And don't worry, it won't be the chapel. I've persuaded them to choose St Saviour's. Much more picturesque.'

It was happening too quickly, and Nancy wanted to put out her hand and apply a brake. 'But—' she began.

'No buts, darling. We've made the big decision and there's no point in delaying. Your parents agree with me.'

Did *she* agree, though? Surely she should have some say? But her parents and Philip were a formidable team, and Nancy felt tired at the thought of the arguments ahead if she disagreed. After all, June was the traditional month for weddings, wasn't it? Even with her limited knowledge, there would be a good many preparations and little time in which to make them.

When she voiced this fear, Philip laughed. 'There's absolutely no need to worry, my sweet. Your mother is bounding with energy. She'll arrange for a choir when she sees the vicar and is happy to order taxis, the photographer, the cake, and she knows an excellent florist in Winchester. She'll take care of all the nitty gritty. And to make you really happy, I've found exactly the right wedding dress for you.'

Nancy's mind was spinning. Was this what it was like when you agreed to marry? No time to enjoy the engagement, no time to choose carefully when and where you married? Everything taken out of your hands? Not everything, she vowed to herself.

'I'm sure you want to spare me a lot of the hard work, but I'd like to choose my own dress, Philip.'

He reached out for her hands and clasped them between his. 'I promise, my darling, the dress will be exactly what you would choose. You will love it.'

Before she could respond, Mrs Minns bobbed out of her doorway and stood, hands on her hips, glaring at them. 'If you've finished, I want to lock up for the night,' she said in a surly voice.

'Of course,' Philip said. 'Mrs Minns, isn't it? I'm so sorry to have inconvenienced you.'

The woman's face softened. In fact, her whole figure appeared to soften and her mouth almost formed itself into a smile. Extraordinary, Nancy thought. She should get Philip to call more often.

Back in her room, though, she found it hard to settle, feeling as restless as she did excited. She was marrying in three months' time! It was difficult to believe. Would telling someone else make it seem more real? Rose—she would tell Rose. Their relationship might not be the same as it once had been, but Rose was the closest friend she had, and it felt right to share this momentous change in her life. Before she slept that night, Nancy wrote a short note, telling her friend she had news and would love to see her.

*

Two days later she received a reply. Rose was coming up

to Oxford Street that very day. Could Nancy meet her after work for a quick cup of tea?

When Nancy walked into the café her friend had mentioned, Rose was sitting at a table by the window.

'So tell me!' she exclaimed, jumping up to greet Nancy. 'What is this big news?'

Nancy sat down and looked across at her friend. 'I'm getting married,' she said.

Rose clapped her hands. 'How wonderful!' And then very quickly, 'To Philip?'

'Only to Philip!' Nancy smiled shyly. 'He's a lovely man, Rose.'

'Of course he is. He couldn't be otherwise. I must meet him immediately. Mike, too. We'll have to arrange that dinner we spoke of. The kids will be in bed and we can talk properly. I want to know this man who's swept you off your feet.'

'And I want *you* to know Philip. He's the best thing that's ever happened to me, Rose. Dinner sounds perfect.'

'Shall we say a week on Saturday? Living where we do can feel like the outer ring of hell, but finding us shouldn't be too difficult. We're at the very end of the tube line. Just around the corner from the station.'

'I'll ask Philip about the date,' Nancy said happily.

'If he's booked for that Saturday, make it the next one. We're always home at weekends, so pick whatever day suits you both.'

'I'm sure a week Saturday will be fine—I can't think anything will clash with it.'

But when Nancy recounted the invitation to her fiancé that Friday evening, he shook his head. 'No can do, darling. Sorry.'

He offered no further explanation and Nancy didn't like to ask. Despite knowing him for almost a year, there were still areas of Philip's life of which she knew little.

'It doesn't matter if we can't make that day. Rose said any Saturday would suit them. How about the following weekend?'

Philip frowned heavily, so much so that for a moment Nancy thought he was angry. But then his face cleared. 'Let's make it that one,' he said, giving her a quick hug.

*

She dressed carefully for Rose's dinner, choosing a light blue wool frock with a Peter Pan collar and a nipped-in waist. Her wardrobe was sparse and she'd bought the dress some years ago, but recently had it brought up-to-date by the dressmaker a work colleague had recommended. Rose wouldn't care what she wore, Nancy knew, but Philip would. He was bound to be as smart as a new pin. He liked to impress, she'd noticed, and he was meeting her friends for the first time. He'd promised to collect her at seven that evening, having reckoned the journey should take them no more than half an hour. Nancy waited at the top of the staircase, listening eagerly for his knock. She needed to get to the door before Mrs Minns.

Seven o'clock passed without Philip's arrival. Then seven fifteen. As the minutes ticked slowly on, Nancy's eagerness faded and concern filled its place. Had Philip been unable to leave work? Nancy still had the number for the newspaper—Philip had given it to her before their very first date. She could walk to the telephone box in the next street and hope he didn't arrive at Chilworth Road in the meantime, but he would hate her to phone him at work. He'd said the number was for emergencies only. Surely if he'd been delayed, he should have telephoned here? Mrs Minns would be annoyed to have her Saturday evening disturbed, but Philip could easily have charmed her.

He should have telephoned, unless… he'd had an accident. The image of her sweetheart lying in a hospital bed, swaddled in bandages, invaded Nancy's mind. Get a grip, she warned herself, he'll be here soon. In the meantime, how was she to warn Rose they would be very late? Other than sending a telegram, she had no way of getting in touch with her friend, and the telegram service would have closed by now.

When ten o'clock struck and there was still no sign of Philip, Nancy began slowly to undress. Poor Rose. Dinner ruined and no explanation. Her friend must feel bewildered, and Nancy felt horribly guilty at letting her down so badly. Tomorrow she must write a note and send profuse apologies. In the meantime, where was Philip?

That night, she hardly slept for worry, waiting on edge for the telephone to ring, expecting any minute a call from the hospital, or the newspaper, or from one of Philip's friends. If he were in trouble, surely he'd have found a way of getting a message to her? But the call never came, and as the night wore on, her mind strayed into ever more troublesome territory. Philip had never wanted to come to dinner, had been reluctant to meet Rose and her family, had refused to introduce Nancy to any of his friends. Was it possible he had deliberately stayed away? No. She couldn't think such a thing of him.

She was up and dressed very early. Early enough to hear knocking at the front door. Philip! At last!

She rushed headlong down the stairs to reach the door before Mrs Minns could intervene, but when she hurried across the hall, there was only silence. Thankfully, the landlady appeared to be sleeping still.

Nancy pulled back the front door, her face tight with worry, but it was Rose who was on the doorstep.

'Are you all right, Nancy?'

'Rose!' she said in a dazed voice. 'How did you find me? And you've come all this way and so early?'

'You gave me your address, remember? I'm sorry if I've woken you.'

'But the children? Where are they?'

'Mike is getting the girls their breakfast and has promised to take them to Sunday school later. I came because I was concerned for you. What happened last night? When you didn't turn up, I was worried sick that you might have had an accident.'

It was a natural reaction; it had been Nancy's worry over Philip. She touched her friend lightly on the arm. 'I'm so sorry to have let you down. The food —' she began.

'The food is nothing, but are you all right?'

'Yes. Fine. It's just that... 'she cast around for an excuse that might sound plausible...'that Philip had to work. He had to meet a deadline,' she finished in a rush, inspiration coming suddenly. 'And I had no way of letting you know.'

'I see.' Rose's lips pursed slightly. 'So when did *you* know?'

'Philip telephoned.'

The lie tripped off Nancy's lips. She couldn't tell the truth—that she had no idea why Philip hadn't come—and felt herself pushed into excusing him.

'I see,' Rose said again. 'And when did he telephone?' She seemed unconvinced by Nancy's explanation.

'I'm not sure exactly. Does it matter?'

'Well, yes, it does. If Philip knew he was going to work late, he could have let you know in good time. And you could have telegrammed me.'

'Perhaps he didn't know until it was too late,' Nancy said wildly.

Rose looked hard at her. 'It all seems a bit odd, Nancy. That he couldn't have told you earlier.'

There was a long pause. Nancy could say nothing more, having lied, it seemed, to no avail.

When Rose spoke again, there was a note of wonder in her voice. 'He didn't tell you, did he? He didn't phone. You had no idea he wasn't coming. The deadline you mentioned is a fantasy.'

'Philip often has a last minute rush.' It was a final attempt to defend her lie. 'I'm sure he would have told me in good time if it was possible.'

'I hope so, otherwise it's a shabby way to treat you. And me.'

'I'm really, really sorry about the confusion last night, Rose, and I'll try to make up for it in some way. I'm sure there's a very good explanation.'

'Maybe. But you're my friend, and I don't like to think you've been treated badly.'

Nancy clasped her friend's hands. 'I love Philip with all my heart. This marriage means so much to me. Please understand.'

Rose paused for a moment, fidgeting from one foot to the other. 'I'm trying to, but are you sure about this engagement?'

Nancy was so desperately upset that right now she wasn't sure of anything. Her night time fear had come alive again, that Philip had deliberately chosen not to come. Once more, she pushed it away. She wouldn't think it and, though Rose had been her best friend, the only friend who'd stood by her throughout a miserable childhood, she heard herself say in a frosty voice, 'Of course I'm sure. What on earth are you suggesting?'

Rose drew herself up, her figure straight and stiff. 'Fine. I hope it all works out for you.' She stepped back from the doorway and turned to go. 'But don't blame me if your precious engagement goes haywire.'

Nancy put out a despairing hand to stop her friend from leaving, but then let it fall to her side. If she was forced to choose, she had to choose Philip.

# Chapter Seven

Nancy dragged herself to work that morning, extremely upset by her friend's strained departure, and bewildered at how quickly events had unfolded. Rose had come to Chilworth Road as a good friend, concerned that Nancy had suffered no serious ill, but she had left as—an adversary? How could that be? Yet it had happened, and Nancy couldn't unsay the things that had been said. Black thoughts haunted her, her face so gloomy that the post boy, throwing a pile of mail onto her desk, couldn't resist a quip.

'Gettin' ready to kill yerself, are yer?' He gave her a cheeky grin.

Nancy felt as though she well might. She had lost the one friendship that meant a great deal to her, and she still had no idea where Philip might be.

Every evening she waited for a phone call and every morning for a letter. But she heard nothing. Ordinarily, she wouldn't think it unusual. Friday was their day for meeting. The same time, the same restaurant run by an Italian family, near Marble Arch. But surely, he should have contacted her by now, and put her mind at rest.

At one point, she felt so uneasy that she risked breaking Abingers' rules and made a personal telephone call to *The Daily Enquirer*. To reach Philip, she was forced to brave several intermediaries, and explain to each of them just why she was ringing, only to be told eventually that he was in a meeting and couldn't be reached. She had never truly believed he was in trouble, but at least now she had the confirmation. There was relief, too, that she hadn't actually managed to speak to him. Philip would have been very unhappy—he'd made it clear that she was only to use the newspaper's number in an emergency.

By the end of the week, she was in two minds whether or not to go to the restaurant. What if Philip wasn't there? What if he'd disappeared from her life entirely? But on Friday, weighed down by a succession of long, unhappy days, she decided to confront whatever lay in wait.

When she arrived at *La Famiglia*, Philip was sitting at their usual table, reading a newspaper. He smiled at her as she hovered in the doorway, then jumped up and pulled out a chair.

'Good timing, Nancy. I hear Signora Martinelli is making a special dish tonight, one that comes from her beloved Tuscany, and she'll have it on the table in a matter of minutes.'

For an instant, Nancy had felt enormous relief that Philip was here. But relief swiftly transformed into bewilderment.

'Are you all right, Philip?' she asked, looking directly into his face.

He seemed surprised. 'Naturally, darling. Why wouldn't I be? But come and sit down.'

'You didn't turn up on Saturday evening and I was worried. I've been worried all week. You never contacted me.'

Philip's eyebrows drew together. 'Saturday evening? I don't recall…'

'We were going to dinner with Rose and Mike. My friends,' she said with emphasis. 'You promised to collect me at seven o'clock that evening.'

'Did I? Do you know, I don't remember. Are you sure?'

'Of course I'm sure.'

He shrugged his shoulders. 'That's unfortunate, darling. It must have slipped my mind.'

Nancy felt for the ruby ring and twisted it fiercely around her finger. 'It was more than unfortunate, Philip. It was rude.'

When he said nothing, she reached across the table and took his hands in a firm grip. 'Rose means a great deal to me. She's my closest friend. She has been most of my life.'

Philip disentangled himself from her grasp. 'I'm sure you'll smooth things over, darling. Say all the right things. But in future, perhaps it's best you make arrangements to see your friend on your own.'

Nancy stared at him and he went on, 'Better still, why not forget her altogether? She belongs in the past, and this is a new chapter in your life. You're with me now. We'll make our own friends together.'

He had dismissed Rose as unworthy of even an apology, and Nancy hated it. Hated that Philip couldn't see how much this friendship meant to her. But she had burned her boats with Rose. She had made her choice.

'Now about this delicious meal the *signora* is serving us, I've ordered a very nice Chianti to go with it.'

Signora Martinelli bustled up to the table at that moment, a dish of bubbling pasta in her hands, while her husband deftly poured the wine. Nancy forced herself to eat, though every mouthful seemed as though it would choke her. Philip talked easily throughout the meal and Rose and her belated dinner were forgotten—though not by Nancy.

Over the next few weeks, though, she wondered if her words had had some effect—had made Philip realise how hurtful his behaviour had been—since he went out of his way to cosset her. There were special trips to the theatre, Sunday lunch at the Ritz no less and, much to Mrs Minns' envy, a bouquet of flowers so enormous the delivery boy could hardly get them through the door.

Nancy had tried several times to write a letter to Rose, but somehow the right words had never come. Now she decided she must put the upset aside and concentrate on her future. A new life beckoned.

*

One evening, she arrived back from Abingers to find a letter from her mother waiting on the shabby chest that served as a hall table. Her parents were coming to London this coming weekend and suggested they meet Nancy and her fiancé for lunch. Nancy raised her eyebrows. Her parents coming to London! It was unheard of. They rarely left Riversley and the furthest they ever travelled was Winchester. It was years since they'd done even that. In his retirement, her father seemed content to spend his days pottering in his allotment, and her mother in good works for the chapel.

When Philip was told of their visit, he decided they would meet in a café near Waterloo, a short walk from the station. Nancy was unsure why the Nicholsons had decided to brave London—her mother had given no explanation in her letter—but it seemed an important occasion and she took time to think what she should wear. The weather had turned warmer this last week and her favourite summer frock, the wine-coloured polka dot, seemed a sensible option. She hadn't worn it since last summer and, slipping the frock over her petticoat, crossed her fingers it would still fit. Perfect! Smoothing out the square neckline, she twirled in front of the old cheval mirror she'd found in the market. The dress looked good, she decided.

Her landlady had gone shopping and Nancy's fellow lodger seemed to sleep most of the weekend, so when the front door knocker sounded, she ran down the stairs to answer it. A delivery man stood on the doorstep.

'Miss Nicholson? This is for you.' He thrust a large rectangular box into her hands and turned to walk back up the path.

'I don't think—' she began, but he was already opening the door of his van.

It must be a mistake. The only thing Nancy had ever had delivered to her were the wonderful flowers Philip had sent. She carried the cardboard box up to her room, checking the label as she did. The parcel was certainly addressed to her. Deciding she'd better open it before she left for the café, she unearthed a pair of scissors from the kitchen drawer, cut the string and peeled back the lid. Sheets of tissue paper greeted her and there, nestled deep in their folds, lay a dress. Carefully, she drew it out. The material was soft and sleek. Silk, Nancy thought. How lovely. But mauve silk. Mauve had never suited her, though she could see the dress itself was beautifully made and must have cost a good deal of money. There was a folded note in the bottom layer of tissue.

*For you, my darling*, it read. *You deserve only the best. Philip.*

How thoughtful of him. And how extravagant. But if only he'd asked, Nancy could have told him that mauve was a shade she never wore. It took the colour out of her face and was deeply unflattering. She would have chosen a quite different hue. A different style, too. This one had a deep décolleté and she would feel uncomfortable wearing it. But Philip had meant only good, and her heart warmed to him.

He was already at the café when she arrived, sitting with her parents at a corner table. He looked up as Nancy made her way over to them, a wide smile on his face. But when he rose to greet her, she saw a frown appear, deepening as she watched, and his mouth seemed suddenly hard and tight.

'Didn't you get the parcel?' he asked abruptly.

'The dress? Yes, it came this morning. I was just about to thank you.' Nancy hadn't had time to sit down, let alone begin thanking him for his present.

'Then why aren't you wearing it?'

'I thought it much too good for this place,' she extemporised. Discussing the unfortunate colour would have to come later.

'But I bought it for you to wear today,' Philip protested. '*I* didn't think it was too good for this café.'

Harry Nicholson had his head buried in the menu, seemingly oblivious to the tension, but Nancy's mother was looking worried, glancing from one to the other of them, trying to understand what was going on.

'A cotton dress is better in this weather,' Nancy said mildly.

'That one, you mean.' There was a hardly hidden contempt in his voice.

'It's a pretty dress,' she said spiritedly, though inwardly she felt her stomach hollow.

'It's cheap and nasty, Nancy. The sort of thing shop girls wear.'

'Is there a problem?' Ruth asked, unusually timorous.

'I bought Nancy a beautiful silk dress, Mrs Nicholson, especially for today. It's not every day you and your husband come to London and I wanted to make the occasion memorable. But it appears she prefers the rag she has on.'

'What a shame,' her mother said reprovingly. 'You should have worn the silk.'

'I can see that now,' Nancy said tautly. 'But I'm here and ready to eat lunch, so perhaps for the moment I can be excused my cheap and nasty dress.'

Philip threw back his head suddenly and laughed. 'You can, my love. But make sure you don't do it again. Thank God, I've chosen your wedding dress.'

'The dress is beautiful, Nancy. So elegant,' Ruth confided. 'It arrived yesterday, and I've hung it in your wardrobe. You will look lovely when you walk down the aisle.'

So her mother had seen the dress she was to wear on her wedding day, but she hadn't?

'It won't look lovely if it doesn't suit me,' Nancy said tartly. 'And certainly not lovely if it doesn't fit. But perhaps in the amazing planning you've all done, no one has thought of that?'

'The dress *will* suit you,' Ruth said complacently. 'I could see that as soon as I unpacked it. As for a good fit, come down to Riversley next weekend and see for yourself. If there should be any problem, and I'm sure there won't be, I'll ask Lilian to call. She is an excellent dressmaker.'

A coil of anger had begun to unfold deep inside Nancy, but she tried hard to maintain a calm face in what had become a topsy-turvy world.

'And the church?' she asked. 'I believe you were going to organise that, too.'

'St Saviour's,' Harry said gruffly, joining the conversation for the first time. 'We didn't much like it, but Philip here says he's Anglican, not chapel, so it's only right.'

'We could have compromised with a register office.'

Three pairs of eyes fixed on her with horror. 'No!' her companions said in unison.

Conversation over the meal was taken up entirely by the wedding and, for the most part, carried on over Nancy's head. Arrangements had been made: flowers, cake, reception, choir, photographer. She could have argued, but it was easier to let it go. Easier to be a coward.

'No bridesmaids, dear,' her mother said. 'You're a little too mature for bridesmaids.'

Just as well, Nancy reflected. She had nobody she could

have asked.

'And Philip has booked the honeymoon. My dear, you will be so pleased,' her mother went on.

'Will I?' she asked brightly, by now ready to scream. 'That is good to know. I wonder, will I be pleased about the best man, too? Or perhaps he's something I *will* be allowed to choose.'

'Don't be silly,' Philip chided. 'It's evident I'm the one who decides on my best man. But he's staying a secret. You won't know who he is until the day.'

She knew very well that the best man was always the bridegroom's choice, and her remark had simply been a feeble attempt to fight back. She had become a puppet, she realised, with no way out of the performance—except to call the whole thing off. She couldn't do that. She loved Philip and wanted to marry him. The wedding was just one day, she comforted herself. When it was over, things would be different.

Her head ached and for the first time she didn't want to be with Philip. She wanted to be alone, back at Chilworth Road, in the room she'd made her home. But it was only when every tiresome detail had been pulled this way and that, and final decisions made, that they were able to leave the café and walk her parents to the station.

## Chapter Eight

A second letter arrived some days later. It was strange, Nancy thought, that months, years, could pass without ever receiving mail and now she'd had two letters in less than a week. Recognising the handwriting on the envelope, her heart gave a flip. It was from Rose.

A sweet letter, too. Her friend apologised for any upset she'd caused. She had been worried about Nancy's safety, she said, and that had made her hasty to judge. Naturally, it was proper that Nancy defended the man she was to marry, and Rose had no right to criticise him. She hoped that they could still be friends; their friendship was too precious to lose.

Nancy read the missive through several times, then tucked it away in her handbag. It was comforting to know that Rose still cared for her, particularly feeling as she did. Friendless. It was irrational, she knew—she was just about to marry—but she couldn't banish the sense of isolation that had begun to take hold. She had thought Philip a true friend, a man whose feelings for her were sincere. A man who would always put her first. But it no longer felt like that. Philip had aligned himself with her parents. She was their puppet and the three of them were busy pulling her strings. Together, they had taken from her the freedom to enjoy the most wonderful day of her life. She'd been allowed no dissent; she was simply expected to go along with everything they'd decided.

But when she met Philip that week for their usual Friday evening, Nancy rebelled. Over a first course of minestrone soup, he began to discuss where they should live after their wedding day.

'A house outside London,' he said. 'It's got to be—property will be so much cheaper.'

She was quick to counter his suggestion. 'That wouldn't really do, though, would it?' 'There's our work to consider.'

'Work's not a problem,' he replied airily. 'I can work from anywhere. Phone in my copy. As long as I get to the office a couple of times a week, my boss will be fine with it. We could rent a lovely house for the same money as a poky flat in Chelsea. But we need to get on with it, Nancy. The wedding is in less than a month.'

'Finding a home is important, I agree, but you haven't considered *my* work. You may be able to work anywhere, but I can't. I'd have to commute every day. It would mean a very early start, a tiring journey, and I've no idea how much train travel would cost. I don't even know if I could afford it on the salary Abingers pay me.'

Philip beamed indulgently. 'My poor love. You mustn't worry. You're about to acquire a husband. I'm the one who'll pay our bills.'

'A season ticket could cost a great deal,' she warned.

'There won't be a train fare to pay, silly. You won't be working.'

Nancy stared at him. 'But I must work.'

He reached out and clasped her hand. 'Not anymore, sweetheart. That's my role. I'll be the breadwinner, and I promise I'll do it well. I'll make sure you have a good life. The happiest life.'

Nancy struggled to find the words. She wanted to say

that work was too important for her simply to abandon it. That if work was part of his life, it must be part of hers. That she didn't want to be a kept woman. That she hated the very thought of negotiating housekeeping, asking for pin money, confessing to bills. It would feel degrading.

Before she could think how best to phrase what she knew would be unpalatable,  Philip continued to talk. 'While your old man slaves away at the typewriter, you'll have your feet up and be enjoying it. Like your mother. Like all married ladies. I want you to have a comfortable life and, until the children come, you can take it easy. That's the way it should be.'

Nancy swallowed hard, trying to keep her voice even. 'Will you excuse me for a moment, Philip? I need to visit the bathroom.'

In the ladies' cloakroom, Nancy stood at the washbasin, hands grasping cold, white porcelain, and looked at herself in the mirror. A long, hard look. Could this really be happening to her? She couldn't let it. She had gone along with her clothes being chosen for her, her wedding arranged without consultation, even her best friend dismissed as unimportant. But she couldn't lose her work. She would dwindle to nothing. And then Philip would no longer love her. Couldn't he see that?

She splashed her face with cold water and tried to breathe deeply. She must stand firm on this point, at least. They would have to live in London, within reach of Abingers, even if they were forced to rent in an area that Philip disliked. She must try to make him understand what her work meant to her. Fortified, she walked out of the bathroom, ready to state her case.

Emerging into the restaurant, their table was straight ahead of her, and she saw that Philip was reading. Not his customary newspaper. Something much smaller. A letter? From the mysterious best man perhaps? But, as she drew closer, she noticed that the handbag she'd left behind was open on the table-top. He had opened her bag and rifled

inside. He'd taken the letter. It was Rose's letter he was reading!

'What are you doing?' she demanded, plumping down on her seat, though what he was doing was patently clear.

'Your friend writes a nice letter, darling.' He calmly folded the two sheets of paper back into their envelope. 'But I'm relieved you're not seeing her anymore. You made a sensible choice. It doesn't do for friends to be involved in a marriage and this, this Rose, clearly wanted to be.' Philip shook his head. 'Doesn't do at all. Causes all kinds of problems between husband and wife.'

'You took my letter.' Nancy still couldn't quite believe it. Not only had Philip stolen the letter from her handbag, but he had shown not the slightest sign of embarrassment when found reading it.

'Yes? What of it?' He smiled across at her.

'That was private correspondence, Philip.' How was she to make him understand how seriously she took his abuse of trust?

'We're getting married. Couples share everything, Nancy. Nothing is private when you're married.'

'So in future you'll feel entitled to read everything that comes to me?'

'Naturally.'

'You'll listen to my telephone calls? Rummage through my cupboards?'

'Absolutely. Why not? Unless you've got something dastardly to hide, you really shouldn't mind.' He was smiling still.

Nancy waited for her heart to stop pounding quite so noisily and then, very deliberately, took the ring from her fourth finger and handed it to him.

'What's this?' He looked confused.

'Your ring, Philip. I'm giving it back to you. I can't go on with this. I can't marry a man who reads my letters, chooses my clothes, decides my friends for me.'

He gave an uncertain laugh. 'This is ridiculous, darling. You don't mean it.'

'I'm afraid I do. I love you, Philip, but I can't live in the way you evidently think right.'

'It's the way every man thinks is right,' he spluttered.

'In that case, I had better not marry at all.'

'You say you love me, yet you give me my ring back. How dare you!' He leaned angrily across the table. 'How dare you,' he repeated. 'A trumped-up assistant in a decrepit auction house. A woman who has never had a boyfriend. Not one that stuck anyway. You were twenty-six when I met you and a million miles from even getting engaged. You should be grateful I bothered to notice you.'

He got up from his seat, his face white. 'Bloody grateful, do you hear?'

And, with that, Philip March stormed out of the restaurant.

# *Chapter Nine*

Nancy wasn't sure how she spent the rest of that weekend. Going through the mundane actions of buying food, cleaning her room, cooking supper? But always, always, consumed by unhappiness. She barely recalled leaving the house on Sunday morning and walking down the Edgeware Road to Hyde Park. It was a lengthy distance, though she hardly noticed. Hardly noticed the families enjoying a bright summer day: paddling a boat on the Serpentine, setting up a makeshift cricket pitch, lazing in the park café, the sun warming their faces. She couldn't stop thinking of Philip, of the decision she'd made. It seemed so momentous. He had been her knight in shining armour and now she had dismissed him forever. How could she have done that?

But the more she thought, the more she questioned — how much of a knight had he really been? Walking aimlessly around the park, she finally admitted the unease she'd felt for weeks, the doubts she'd refused to acknowledge, burying them deep. Her discomfort had started the day Philip had forgotten the dinner with Rose. Except that he hadn't forgotten, Nancy was certain. Instead, he'd decided quite deliberately not to go. When he'd told her that it was best he didn't meet her friends, what he'd really meant was that he didn't want her to have friends that weren't his.

And he hadn't wanted her to meet any of *his* friends. He'd made no attempt to introduce her to anyone who was part of his life—friends, work colleagues, not even his parents. He'd told her they lived in the north of Scotland and the journey was too difficult.

How had she got to this point? By forgiving and forgetting? By deliberately making herself blind? When she hadn't worn the unsuitable mauve dress, she had dismissed his anger as a natural reaction: Philip had felt his generosity thrown back at him, she'd reasoned. When he'd made every wedding arrangement over her head, she'd convinced herself that he was doing so to save her trouble and that things would be different once the day had come and gone.

But Philip's blithe assumption that, when married, she wouldn't work—that she'd be happy for him to keep her— had been a watershed. It had made her realise just what her life had come to. No discussion, simply an assumption. That was how it worked. They didn't discuss—her clothes, the wedding, her job—he assumed, and she was required to go along with it.

And then the crunch. The moment she had seen him reading Rose's letter, she'd had had a blinding vision of what her married life would truly be like. A constant trimming of her principles, a constant reshaping of her priorities, of her life itself, all to suit Philip. It was a frightening future. Even more frightening was his true nature, revealed in all its starkness in that final, vile onslaught when, incredulous, he'd realised that she was serious in giving back his ring.

How could she have been so mistaken in a man? She had to look deep inside and what she saw gave her no comfort. It was pride. From the moment Philip had spoken to her outside Westminster Abbey, she'd been a slave to it. Pride that she had found a man of her own. Pride that someone as good-looking and clever and well-connected as Philip liked her well enough to ask her out. Then loved her well enough to ask her to marry. She'd been seduced by pride.

But seduced, too, by her need to love and be loved. It had been a gaping absence in her life and, finding Philip, she had basked in the knowledge that for the first time, to someone, she was the most precious person in the world. And that, in finding him, she had at last pleased her parents.

It was the following Sunday evening that her father arrived. Mrs Minns answered the front door and trailed up the stairs to call Nancy, her face filled with suspicion.

'It's my father, Mrs Minns,' Nancy said, when she saw who was waiting for her in the hall.

The landlady sniffed and went back to her television, while Harry Nicholson puffed his way slowly up three flights of stairs to his daughter's room.

When he recovered his breath, he looked around him. 'Well, I must say you've made it look quite cheerful. Small but cheerful.'

It was unlikely praise and Nancy savoured it. She'd tried hard to make an unprepossessing room homely, spending scarce savings on any simple comfort she could afford. Gingham cotton bought in a sale and sewn into curtains, along with cushions that matched. New china and new cutlery from the corner store and, to brighten the walls, several pictures she'd found in the attics at Abingers which Mr Harker had allowed her to take home, since no one had claimed them for the last thirty years. And then there was the sofa. She'd saved for over a year for it— deep blue velvet, large and luxurious.

'This is very comfortable.' Her father plumped himself down on the sofa. 'This must have cost a bit. Where did you get the money? Philip, I suppose.'

'No,' she said with suppressed anger, any warm feelings

abandoned. 'Not Philip. I bought it from my salary.'

'The auction house—what are they called, Abingers?—they must be paying you well.

'They're not.'

Already Nancy wanted him gone. 'Why are you here, Dad?' she asked.

'I thought you might like to see your old father.' Harry Nicholson had decided to be jovial, but it didn't suit him.

'You never come to London and you've never visited me before. There must be a reason.' She pulled out a wooden kitchen chair and sat looking at him. Something was brewing, something bad, and she wanted it out and dealt with.

'It's about this Philip business.' Her father cleared his throat and looked down at his feet.

'Yes?'

'Your mother and I, we don't want to interfere,' he began.

'That's good news, so let's not talk about it,' Nancy said quickly. 'Can I get you a cup of tea? You must be thirsty.'

'No tea, thank you. Like I say, we don't want to interfere, but I've come to say something and say it I will. Philip March is a splendid chap. A man deserving of respect. And by all accounts, you're not giving him it.'

'By whose account?'

'Well, Philip's,' he admitted. 'The poor chap telephoned us. Most upset and I don't blame him. *We* don't blame him. To hand him back his ring like that. Play fast and loose with a man's affections. It's not worthy of you, Nancy.'

It was clear that Philip had her parents enslaved and intended to keep them that way.

'I'm not playing fast and loose,' she said. 'When I broke the engagement, I gave Philip my reasons. And since I've had time to think more, I've come to doubt he knows any true affection. I think he only likes people as a reflection of himself.'

'I don't understand your fancy words,' Harry said gruffly. 'But I do understand a promise, and you made him one, Nancy. Promised to marry him and now you've torn it up.'

Nancy got up and walked over to the sofa, bending over her father. 'I was mistaken, Dad. Mistaken in him. Philip March is not the man I want to marry.'

'But why not?' Her father was bewildered.

'He wants to possess me, control my life completely, and I can't live with that.'

'Because he buys you a dress?' Her father had noted that little scene at least, she thought.

'Not just because of that. He decides everything—when we marry, how we marry, where we'll live. Even if I can go to work.'

Harry heaved himself to his feet and stood facing her. 'It's natural that he does, Nancy. That's a man's role.'

'In your book, maybe. But not in mine. When I marry, I want an equal relationship.'

'When you marry?' her father burst out. 'You'll be lucky ever to be asked again, my girl. You were bloody lucky to get Philip.'

Nancy had rarely heard her father swear. It was a mark of how disappointed he was. He paused at the door. 'You're knocking on, my dear. You won't get another chance. Best to think again. Philip is a forgiving kind of chap, I'm sure. Tell him you didn't mean what you said—that it was just wedding nerves—and do it very soon. And come down to Riversley next weekend. Your mother needs a chat with you.'

Nancy had a good idea of how the chat would go: her mother in uncompromising mood, issuing commands of what her daughter should say and do to retrieve the fiancé she'd pushed away. She would stay clear of Riversley as long as possible.

But she couldn't entirely. The next evening, she had barely walked through the front door, when the telephone rang, her mother on the other end of the line. At least Mrs Minns wasn't at home to scowl and sniff. Monday evening was when she met her cronies in the local public house and her landlady had evidently left early.

'What on earth have you done?' her mother began. Ruth Nicholson's exasperation was plain. 'What is the matter with you, Nancy? You have the opportunity to marry a professional man, who will keep you in comfort for the rest of your life, and you've whistled him down the wind. What more do you want?'

'Someone who doesn't consider me his possession.'

'You're talking nonsense. Philip is a kind man. He's polite, considerate. He cares deeply for you.'

'He is polite, I agree, but only to get what he wants. He's not so polite when he's thwarted. And really, he doesn't care for me. The person he cares for is himself.'

'How can you say that?' Nancy could hear her mother breathing heavily. 'After everything he's done for you. The places he's taken you, the treats he's showered on you. I've never told you, but he even offered to share the expenses of the wedding.'

He would, wouldn't he? Nancy thought. It was entirely his wedding. But this was something practical she could grasp in trying to make her mother understand that the engagement was truly at an end.

'There won't be a wedding,' she said firmly.

'You can't do this, Nancy. Not to him. Not to us.'

'I'm doing it for me. Can't you see that?'

It was obvious Ruth couldn't, because she continued, 'You

need to write to him. Tell him you were mistaken. Wedding nerves, that's what it is,' she said in an echo of her husband. 'Tell him you're genuinely sorry and it won't happen again. Ask him to forgive you. I know he will. He truly loves you.'

'But, Mum, I've done nothing wrong. I don't need forgiveness.'

'You'll need ours, my girl. We've told everyone in the village that you're to marry next month and now you say you won't go ahead with it.' Her mother almost choked with feeling. 'Do you know that we've already had wedding presents sent here? What do I do with them? What do I say to people?'

'I'm sure you'll think of something.' Nancy's anger was close to erupting. 'You could always try telling them the truth. That the person your daughter mistakenly agreed to marry is an unpleasant, controlling man.'

'You're mad. Completely mad. Philip March is a wonderful man. And don't think we'll sit idly by and let you carry on like this. You need to grovel to him. Make amends in some way. Until you do, we've no wish to see you at Riversley. Have we, Harry?' she asked over her shoulder, as Nancy heard the faint sound of her father's shuffle to the telephone.

Harry Nicholson spoke into the receiver, saying awkwardly, 'It would be much easier, Nancy, if you gave it a go.'

# Chapter Ten

'Are you all right, Miss Nicholson?'

It was Leo Tremayne, carrying a stack of files along the wide first floor corridor. He was looking down at her, concern in his eyes. Hunched over a trestle table, Nancy was in the final stages of sorting proofs for the catalogue she'd planned. Her face, she thought, must be a picture of unhappiness for the professor to look so worried. And she was unhappy. Desperately so. She had tried but failed to push her parents' decree from her mind: *You are not welcome at Riversley until you've made peace with Philip.*

She managed a wobbly smile. 'I'm fine, Professor Tremayne. Just a little tired.'

'Too much fun over the weekend perhaps?'

'That's it,' she agreed, giving an unconvincing laugh.

'I wonder…when you've got your catalogue shipshape, would you mind helping me sort these?' He pointed to the sheaf of files he was carrying. 'One of your young men on the advertising desk has asked me to choose a poster. It's for a forthcoming sale—for a former client of mine. At one time or another, I chose most of the pictures going under the hammer, and I feel some responsibility for the success of the sale. But these are all so good.' He rested the heap of posters on the trestle. 'I'm darned if I can choose.'

Nancy had been about to retreat to her top floor eyrie, but this would be a better distraction. And the professor was good company. She shuffled the final pages of the catalogue into place and said, 'I'd love to help.'

While they leafed their way through the various sketches, Leo Tremayne talked about his client, the scope of his collection, the work he was currently interested in and why the sale was important to him.

'Do *you* paint?' Nancy asked him shyly.

'I used to. My mother was an artist and she taught me. But university, the war, then work, forced me to put it aside. And now the job I do leaves little time.'

'It's a shame you've not been able to continue.'

'It's life, isn't it? But what about you, Miss Nicholson?'

'Nancy, please,' she said, emboldened.

'That's a very pretty name. Do you paint?'

'A little, when I have the time, but not very much now. I went to art school for two years and loved it. It made me realise, though, that I was never going to be good enough as an artist to make a living.'

He sighed. 'Very few are. It's hugely competitive. Working here seems a sensible alternative.'

'It might be, if I could do what I'd really like,' she said unguardedly.

Leo looked at her intently. 'And what's that?'

'I shouldn't have said that. It doesn't matter. What do you think of this one? It seems a little different, more arresting than the others.'

The professor turned the poster in his hand and nodded. 'You're right. You have an artist's eye, Nancy.'

That evening she still felt buoyed enough by the encounter to begin again on renovating her room. As a start, she cleaned it from top to tail. Tomorrow, when she returned home, she would find the pot of paint she'd stored at the back of a cupboard and repaint the walls. The room had always needed a second coat, but for the last year, she'd been too bound up with Philip to think of doing it. Now seemed the right time. It will mark a new beginning, she thought. My parents have made their decision, but I've made mine. Cut off from the little support she'd ever had, Nancy still felt brave. She could do this.

\*

It was Thursday when she saw Philip March again. She had finished painting her room the evening before, working into the small hours, and decided that for the next few days she had earned a rest. She would call at the local library on her way home and choose a book in which to lose herself.

She got off the bus at a stop nearest the library and walked swiftly, the summer evening cool and threatening rain. Nearing the entrance, she was aware of footsteps following her, a figure close behind, but turned into the library without looking back. It took her some time to find the right book — it was a while since she'd done any serious reading — and by the time she pushed through the library's swing doors again, it had begun to rain.

It had been a fine day earlier and she hadn't bothered to carry an umbrella, so she stood for a while in the covered porch, hoping the rain would ease. Gradually, she became conscious that she was sharing the space with someone else. Someone hardly visible in the dark shadows cast by stone pillars on either side of her. It was then she remembered the footsteps. Had she been followed? It wasn't likely, but she felt uneasy, and decided she'd be well-advised to brave the downpour.

As soon as she made a move forward, she felt a hand on

her arm, gripping her tightly, and a voice she knew well.

'Not leaving already, Nancy? You'll be soaked.'

'Hallo, Philip.' She tried to sound calm. 'Please let go of me.'

'I might, when we've had our little chat.'

'Why are you here? What do you want with me?'

Her mind was busy. How had he traced her here? He knew her route home from Abingers, but she had got off the trolley bus two stops earlier than usual, which meant he must have followed her all the way from work.

He let go of her arm but planted himself in front of her, effectually barring her way. 'Like I said, I want to talk to you. Talk some sense into you.'

'If the talk is about marriage, please don't. It will lead to unhappiness for us both and I'd like to stay friends. Or acquaintances,' she amended.

'Acquaintances? You have changed your tune. A week ago, you couldn't wait to be my wife.'

'Perhaps I wasn't as eager as you thought,' she said. In the darkening light, she saw fury in his face. 'If I've misled you, I'm truly sorry, but I no longer wish to marry.'

'I don't buy the "misled", and I can't quite work out why you think you have a choice.'

Nancy gaped at him.

'You made a promise,' he continued, echoing her father's words the previous weekend. 'You promised to marry me. The wedding is arranged. June the eighth is now two weeks away. Rather than reading library books, shouldn't you be getting ready?'

'For what? There will be no wedding and, if you haven't yet spoken to the vicar, you really should. You made the arrangements— it's surely your responsibility to cancel them.'

It was as though she hadn't spoken. 'There's a hair

appointment, for instance. You'll want to see a hairdresser that day and they do get booked up. Unless, of course, you want me to book that, too. Or maybe you'd prefer I styled it for you.' He spoke with a false humour that made Nancy's stomach curdle.

'I won't be making any hair appointment.' She tried to keep her voice even. 'I won't be attending any wedding. Our engagement is over. Please accept that.'

'You're wrong, Nancy. Very wrong.' He pushed up close to her so that she could feel the warmth coming off his body. 'It's not over. You would be wise to take this back.' He unfurled his palm to show the ruby ring nestling against his skin, blood red and gleaming wickedly at her.

'It's a beautiful ring, but I won't be wearing it. Now if you'll allow me to pass…'

March made to grab her arm, but at that instant a woman walking her dog paused at the library entrance and stared hard at them, forcing him to drop his grasp. Nancy took her chance. She slid out of the porch and walked quickly away, keeping in the lee of the unknown dog walker. Philip made no attempt to follow. He wouldn't want to expose himself as the bully he was, Nancy thought, not even to an anonymous passer-by.

But her relief at escaping his venom was short-lived.

Only days later, he appeared at her shoulder while she was buying fruit from a market stall.

'You made a promise to me,' he hissed in her ear. 'You're lucky that I'm willing to overlook your strange behaviour. But it has to stop. You've had your little joke and the wedding is too close for you to continue this stupidity.'

His face was set and his eyes cold. 'I expect you to fulfil your promise, or—'

'Or what?'

Nancy sounded combative, demanding an answer, though it was clear there wouldn't be one. Reason played no part in whatever was going on in Philip's mind. He was a man obsessed.

'You'll find out what, if you persist in rejecting me.'

Picking up the bag of apples she'd bought, Nancy dodged beneath his outstretched arm and quickly lost herself in the crowd. That Philip March was intent on vengeance was plain, but the form it might take remained a frightening question mark.

Over the next few weeks, every ounce of her energy was concentrated on finding ways to avoid him. It wasn't easy. He dogged her footsteps, appearing out of nowhere on the pavement in front of her or emerging suddenly from shop doorways. And despite the wedding date having passed, there was always the same angry refrain on his lips. Nancy was in a constant state of tension, always looking over her shoulder, always stopping at blind corners while she gathered the courage to walk on.

One evening, he caught the same bus as her, slipping into the next seat. 'Because of your foolishness, I've had to postpone the wedding. But the vicar has told me of a cancellation in August and your parents are happy with the new date. We'll marry then. August is only weeks away, though. You need to be ready.'

Nancy said nothing, but pushed past him and ran down the stairs to the lower deck, jumping from the bus the minute it slowed. Life had become unnerving. In a few short weeks, Philip had transformed from the man she was to marry into her tormentor, a man conducting a deliberate war of nerves against her. He was her enemy now and the realisation was sickening.

And he was succeeding in his war. Nancy had become

forgetful: mislaying a sugar bowl, finding her shoes where she didn't recall leaving them, thinking she had dumped rubbish in the bin when she hadn't. She was so tense that she began to forget things at work, too, and was twice reprimanded by Mr Harker for bringing him the wrong documents to sign.

Today, she must ensure these particular forms, destined for Aubrey Simmonds, were correct. She went through the file of papers again, ticking off the forms one by one against the list she'd been given and, when she was satisfied, took them to the chief curator's office. Leo Tremayne was sitting in the leather-covered guest chair and greeted her warmly.

Simmonds raised his eyebrows. 'Leave them there, Miss Nicholson,' he said brusquely.

She did as she was bid, but halfway down the corridor on her way back to the stairs, she heard a noise behind her. When she turned, she saw Leo Tremayne hurrying to catch her up.

'I'm going out for a cup of coffee,' he said. 'I've tried your cafeteria but—'

'The coffee tastes like ditch water,' she finished for him.

He laughed. 'Superior ditch water, naturally. But will you join me?'

'I should be getting back to my office—'she started to say.

'It's eleven o'clock. You're allowed a short break, aren't you? We'll be no more than fifteen minutes. I know a good place around the corner.'

The professor had a kind face and kindness was in short supply. Nancy nodded and followed him down the flight of marble stairs and through the swing doors to the road outside.

The café was a few minutes' walk, down a narrow side street. She had never noticed it before, despite working at Abingers for nearly ten years. Too busy, she thought. And Leo Tremayne was right. The coffee was excellent, hot and strong, and ready within minutes.

He half finished his cup before he spoke. 'I hope you don't mind my saying this, but you look very tired still. When I asked you before, you said you were fine, but are you sure you're all right?' His deep brown eyes were full of concern.

'I've a few problems at the moment,' Nancy said. 'That's all.'

'If they're personal and you don't want to talk about them, please don't. But if I can be of any help, tell me.'

'Not really, but thank you.' Nancy stirred her coffee, put the spoon down, then stirred again. 'It's my fiancé,' she said at last.

'I didn't realise you were engaged.' She saw him give her bare fingers a brief scan.

'I'm not anymore. That's the problem. The man I was engaged to won't let me go.'

It sounded dramatic but it was how it felt, as though she were caught between the jaws of a vice.

Leo leaned forward. 'What form does this not letting go take?'

'Constant confrontation, I suppose you'd call it. He appears at odd times—places I'm not expecting him—then harangues me, insisting I promised to marry him and I have to keep the promise. He's even boarding my bus in the evening. There's nowhere I feel free of him.'

The professor sat back in his chair and stretched his legs. 'You need to report him to the police.'

'And what will they do?'

He frowned. 'I'm sure that if you're being harassed by a man, by anyone, they will look into it and warn the person off.'

Nancy doubted the police would take her accusation seriously. They were almost certain to put it down to a lovers' quarrel and not wish to get involved. There were precious few safeguards for women targeted by jealous, angry men.

Leo took another sip of his coffee. 'Can you vary the way you go home perhaps? Maybe take the underground instead—or get off at a different bus stop.'

She didn't like to tell him that she'd thought of all those things, but if Philip March was watching her come and go from work, he wouldn't be shaken off.

'I'll try,' she said, giving what she hoped was a convincing smile.

Leo smiled back, satisfied, it seemed, that he had solved her problem.

# Chapter Eleven

For the next week Nancy did as Leo had suggested in the faint hope it might work. She took the underground and varied her bus routes, though it often meant a much longer walk. One night she walked the entire three miles home, having slipped out of the back entrance of Abingers. But there were no further confrontations, and slowly she began to breathe more easily, each day leaving her home feeling a little more cheerful. As far as she could tell, Philip had stopped following her.

Professor Tremayne hadn't visited Abingers since Nancy had sat with him in the café. She missed seeing him. But she was aware he was an important man, a respected expert who worked abroad a good deal of the time, valuing paintings for wealthy clients and advising galleries and museums across the globe. It appeared a dazzling life.

Her world was far more mundane, but now the Philip problem appeared to have gone away, she settled herself to work harder than ever. And it was work she enjoyed. There was always a chance, a very slight chance to be honest, that she might progress in her chosen department. Wherever possible she volunteered to help with jobs that weren't strictly her responsibility, thinking that the more things she could turn her hand to, the more likely it was that she would climb the mythical ladder.

Fine Art was where she wanted to be. Books were well enough, but it was painting that really set her on fire. It always had been. Recognising that she would never be more than a mediocre artist herself had made Nancy a passionate advocate for painters who were truly gifted. And working at one of the most prestigious auction houses, she was privileged to see great art on a daily basis. When, on occasion, Abingers was asked to sell a particularly hallowed artist—a Gainsborough or a Turner—the sale room was enthralling.

Today she had worked late, helping Mr Harker reorganise a batch of labels, not for the sale room, but for an exhibition. Exhibitions at Abingers were infrequent, but the auction house would occasionally feature an up-and-coming artist and invite potential buyers to browse with a view to purchasing away from the sale room.

This particular display was to showcase the work of a young woman painter, only just becoming known in the art world. The printers, however, had made a complete muddle of titles and prices, and the exhibition was scheduled to open in two days' time. Mr Harker, who had promoted the artist to his superiors as worthy of a show, was exasperated, his temper close to danger point. When Nancy offered to stay behind and sift the labels into some kind of order for a reprint the following day, he was delighted to accept. It was unlikely to bring her any benefit, but she was keen that the work of a new female artist receive the best possible launch.

By the time she arrived home, Nancy was too tired to cook. She made herself a sandwich and a cup of tea, listening with only half an ear to the radio. Then fell exhausted into bed. It would be another busy day tomorrow: a stack of unfinished work, and now a visit to the printers, followed by the relabelling of each canvas in the exhibition. She desperately needed to sleep.

It must have been the small hours when she heard a loud banging. Stumbling out of bed, she opened the door a crack to see Mrs Minns standing there, her hair curlers at an odd angle and her face furious.

'There's a phone call for you,' she said. 'Some bloke.'

'My father?' Nancy felt her stomach tighten at the thought that one of her parents had been taken seriously ill.

'How do I know?' Mrs Minns asked belligerently. 'But it better be an emergency.' She thumped down the stairs ahead of Nancy, disappearing into her bedroom and slamming the door behind her.

The battered grandmother clock struck three as Nancy shivered in the cold of the hall. She felt an inner shiver, too. It had to be bad news.

'Hello,' she said faintly.

'Hello,' she repeated.

Then once more, a little louder, 'Hallo.'

Silence was the only response. Was there someone there? Or perhaps it was a mistake? Someone had phoned this number in error. But then why didn't they say so? After Nancy said another 'hello', she heard a decided click at the other end as the receiver was replaced.

She was mystified and discomfited. Making her way back to her room, she tried to puzzle out what might have happened. But then felt too tired to worry. Mrs Minns had gone back to sleep, and she would, too.

\*

In the morning, as she left the house, the landlady caught her. 'Was that your father on the phone in the night?' she demanded. Then in a softer voice, 'Your family in trouble?'

It was the first kind question the woman had ever asked.

'I hope not, Mrs Minns. It wasn't my father, but I don't know who it was.'

The woman scowled, any kindness vanished. 'Make sure it doesn't happen again.'

How Nancy was supposed to do that, she had no idea. Crossing her fingers it was a rogue call, she caught the bus at the end of the road and was soon immersed in the day's work.

Two nights later, there was another loud bang on her door, if anything even louder.

'I dunno what's going on.' Mrs Minns planted herself astride the doorway, arms folded against her breast. 'But it's some Scottish bloke on the phone this time. This can't go on, Miss Nicholson.'

Nancy felt her heart sink. She knew no one who spoke with a Scots accent and, when she lifted the receiver to say hello, she knew there would be no response. And there wasn't. When it happened on a third night, she said loudly and firmly, 'The police know about you and are listening. If you continue with these calls, be ready to find them on your doorstep.'

It was nonsense, but it was all she could think to say that might frighten the man away.

*

The next morning, the landlady was waiting for her again, this time with a letter in her hand.

'This is your notice.'

'What?' Nancy said, aghast.

'I can't be doing with it. I don't know what you're up to, but I won't be woken in the middle of the night. And I won't be involved in anything bad—this is a respectable house.'

'I'm not involved in anything bad, Mrs Minns. Honestly. I've no idea who is playing these tricks on me.'

'On me, you mean.' Her landlady's tight curls seemed to frizz with anger.

'On both of us,' Nancy corrected herself.

She had a very good idea of the perpetrator, but to name Philip March would achieve nothing. He would be enjoying himself, she thought, confident that he was spreading alarm, hoping no doubt he could force her from her home. She wondered what accent he would adopt when he telephoned again.

'Please take this back.' She offered the letter to her landlady. 'I promise I'll stay up all night, if necessary, to answer any call.'

Mrs Minns snorted, but appeared to hesitate.

'I'll get to the phone before you hear even one ring,' Nancy said, a desperate note in her voice. Her room at Chilworth Road was too precious. The rent was one she could manage, and whatever money she'd had spare, she'd spent on making the place a home. She couldn't begin again somewhere else.

After a long pause, Mrs Minns took back the letter. 'If I'm woken once more, mind, it's out you go, Miss Nicholson.'

That night and for the next few, Nancy stayed up, curled at the bottom of the stairs, a counterpane wrapped around her. It was ridiculous, she thought. How long could she go on like this? She was barely sleeping. When on the fourth night, in a befogged state, she tumbled off the stairs and onto the cold linoleum, she gave up. She would have to risk sleeping in her room. Her work was suffering. She had made numerous mistakes this week, causing Mr Harker to look at her askance and, on one occasion, to reprimand her severely. Even the slightest chance of promotion had been lost.

She went to bed that night in turmoil, expecting to receive an eviction notice in the morning. But when she woke, the clock showed seven and there had been no enraged Mrs

Minns at her door. And no telephone call. Her heart did a little jump. Was it over? When a week had passed and she'd slept without interruption, Nancy decided it was.

The phone calls might be over—presumably Philip had been scared off by the mention of the police, or he'd decided the calls weren't worth the effort of staying up half the night, since so far he'd failed to render her homeless—but Nancy had no illusions that he would stop at this. When he'd given up following her, she'd thought erroneously that he'd abandoned his persecution. But all it had signified was that he'd changed tack, and this would be similar. She wouldn't make the same mistake twice. Philip March was almost certainly planning some other wickedness, and she had to get him to stop.

Would her parents have sufficient influence to persuade him, Nancy wondered? Philip was still in touch with them, it seemed, and she decided it would be worth the difficult reception she'd receive at Riversley, if she could get them to talk him out of this senseless campaign against her. Ruth Nicholson had made it plain that she didn't want to see her daughter until she was back with her fiancé. But if her parents knew what he was doing to her, surely she would have their support?

When she walked into Abingers the next morning, Professor Tremayne was in the foyer. He seemed to be waiting for someone.

'How are you, Nancy?' he greeted her.

'Well, thank you, Professor.'

'Leo, please.' He was looking at her with a slight frown on his face. Evidently one decent night's sleep had not erased the ravages of the last week.

He lowered his voice so that he was speaking almost into her ear. 'Are you still suffering harassment?' he asked tentatively.

'Not so much now,' Nancy prevaricated. She couldn't tell him about the phone calls and Mrs Minns and sleeping on the stairs. It was too humiliating.

He nodded. 'Good. I'm glad. I wonder, have you time for a coffee this morning?'

Nancy's face must have expressed the surprise she felt, because he rushed to say, 'I expect you're too busy. It was stupid of me.'

The truth was that she'd felt too confused by his suggestion to give an immediate answer. Professor Tremayne was only a degree less than royalty in the auction house and here he was asking her to have coffee with him again. Was it possible he'd been waiting in the foyer for *her*?

As Nancy grappled for something to say, Brenda Layton emerged from the lift and walked past them to reach her desk. 'If you've nothing to do, Nancy, I can find you a few jobs,' she said in a spiteful voice, glaring first at Nancy, then pinning on a false smile for the professor.

'I'll let you get on then.' Leo was clearly disappointed.

Nancy smiled a goodbye, before making for the stairs to the upper floors. She felt regretful. She would have liked to spend time with him. He was a decent man, an honourable man, and it would have done her good to talk. Leo Tremayne, she thought, would never make anyone's life a misery.

But she was going to put an end to the misery. Tomorrow was Saturday and she would take the train to Riversley, spend a night there, and be back in London early on Sunday. She had no way of warning her parents that she was coming— she dared not ask Mrs Minns if she could use the phone— but when she thought about it, it was probably best that she didn't. She would simply arrive on the doorstep and hope to be let in.

## Chapter Twelve

When Nancy's father opened the bungalow's front door, his face was a study. He seemed unsure whether to be glad or sorry to see his daughter.

'Who is it, Harry?' his wife called from the kitchen.

'Have you done what I told you, Nancy?' he muttered. 'If not, you'd better leave.'

'I need to talk to you, Dad. Both of you.'

'Who is it?' her mother asked again, coming to peer over his shoulder, a wooden mixing spoon in her hand.

'She wants to talk, Ruth,' her father said gruffly.

'Really? There's only one thing I want to talk about, and she's set her face against it. There's no welcome here for you, Nancy.'

'Philip is what I want to talk to you about,' Nancy said quickly, hoping the name would be sufficient to allow her inside.

It seemed that it was because her mother stepped back, pulling Harry with her. 'You better come in then. Let's hope you've seen the error of your ways.'

While her mother clattered china in the kitchen, Nancy walked into the sitting room and perched on the edge of the sofa. Her father joined her in the room but didn't take a seat, instead walking awkwardly back and forth, unable it seemed to speak.

Tea arrived and Nancy was handed a cup. 'Well?' her mother asked.

'I need your help,' she said baldly.

'To make up with Philip? Thank goodness, you've seen sense.' Her mother gave a satisfied smile.

'Not to make up with him, Mum,' Nancy was swift to say. 'To stop him doing the things he's doing.'

Ruth banged her cup down on the coffee table's Formica. 'What things? What are you talking about? And why are you here? We both told you not to come, didn't we? Unless you'd changed your ways, and you obviously haven't. We're deeply disappointed in you, Nancy, to treat a decent man the way you have. You'll find no shelter here.'

'I don't want shelter,' Nancy said, her voice trembling. 'I want my life back. Philip March is a monster.'

Her mother jumped up and snatched the cup from Nancy's hand. 'I'll hear no more of this. You can go right now.'

'Philip has been following me. Threatening me. And he's been making anonymous phone calls in the middle of the night. Please help. You could. He telephones you, I know, and when he speaks to you next, please ask him to stop.'

Ruth stood stock still, staring down at her daughter. 'I thought you'd gone a bit batty, behaving the way you have, but now I'm convinced. Threatening you? Making anonymous calls? The heavy breathing kind, I take it,' her mother said sarcastically. 'If someone *is* doing that, you need to tell the police, but don't blacken a good man's name.'

'It's him, Mum. He phones at three in the morning and then says nothing. But he's angered my landlady and if he does it again, I'll be evicted.'

'Have you ever heard such rubbish, Harry?' Ruth appealed to her husband. 'Philip follows her, then makes threatening phone calls?'

'Who else would phone me in the middle of the night and then not speak?'

'Anyone. There are cranks everywhere, Nancy,' her father put in mildly.

'But not a crank who knows it's a shared telephone and that my landlady is—'

'Another monster, I suppose,' her mother finished.

'Mrs Minns isn't a monster,' Nancy said, as calmly as she could. 'But neither is she filled with human charity. She's furious that she's been woken night after night and, if it goes on, I'll be looking for another room.'

'Have the calls gone on'? Her father was looking worried.

'No. Not for a while.'

'Then it *was* some crank,' her father said.

Her mother was still staring at her. 'A crank, but you'd rather blame the man who loves you. There's something wrong with you, Nancy. I've always suspected it. I didn't want to, my own daughter, but you've always had to be different. And it's clear this Philip business has turned your mind completely.'

Her father shook his head. 'You need to apologise to the poor chap, like I told you. And if there is a crank making trouble, Philip's the man to sort it out for you.'

Nancy dug her fingernails into her palms. 'How am I to convince you? There's no crank. It's Philip making the trouble and, though the calls seem to have stopped for the moment, there will be something else. He is persecuting me. Can't you see that? He can't bear that he's been rejected and he's punishing me for it.'

Her mother walked to the sitting room door and opened it wide. '*You* deserve to be punished, for sure. I'm not prepared to hear another word, and neither is your father. Until you can sing a different song, you're not welcome here. Now, please go.'

Staring moodily through the window on the train back to London, Nancy realised it was hopeless. There would be no help from her parents. They had been so thoroughly seduced by Philip that they couldn't see the man beneath the façade. And it was a façade—the formal suit, the doffed hat, the ready smile. A façade that masked an ego so fragile that, as she'd told her mother, he couldn't bear the thought that someone had dared to reject him.

She arrived home late that evening with a blank Sunday in front of her, and far too many spare hours to think over what had happened. She had never been close to her parents, but their refusal to believe her was devastating. Why would they take the word of a man they hardly knew over their own daughter's? Was Philip March so powerful? Nancy felt alone and friendless, more so than at any time since she'd arrived in London.

She was toasting a second slice of bread when she hit on the idea of meeting Rose again. She had never answered her friend's letter, thinking it best to leave things as they were. But since then her life had become a quagmire. Should she confide in Rose, she wondered? Tell her what was happening, ask her advice?

The next morning she spent a considerable time crafting a letter to her friend, this time finding the words a little easier, now that she'd heard from Rose and knew herself forgiven. After apologising for the delay in replying, she spent time asking after Rose and her family, and ended by hinting that things had changed in her life and that she'd be glad to talk it over. She sealed the envelope before she realised she'd run out of stamps. That would be for tomorrow, she thought, placing the letter on the kitchen table, ready to send.

But the envelope was to remain unposted.

Unknown to Nancy, the next blow had already fallen when she walked through the doors of Abingers on Monday morning. If she had noticed colleagues looking at her a little oddly of late, or murmuring in small groups that broke up as she appeared, it had been only vaguely. Abingers was a large firm, spread over four floors of an impressive building, and many of the people working there were unknown to her. Perhaps it wasn't surprising then that she didn't at first notice the sideways looks, colleagues glancing at her beneath their eyelashes, whispers as she passed.

It wasn't until she was in the cafeteria queueing for lunch that she heard it. Her tray was laden. It was a particularly nice meal that day and she'd chosen the beef and roast potatoes with apple tart and custard to follow. She was waiting to pay when there was some kind of kerfuffle at the till, slowing the queue down. Nancy stood for some while waiting her turn.

It was then she heard someone behind her say, 'Is that her at the front?' It was one of the Oxbridge graduates that Abingers specialised in. Nancy recognised the exaggerated accent.

'Yeah,' another voice answered. 'The bigwigs can't have heard yet. Once they do, they'll have to dump her.'

'Or she'll be setting up a knocking shop on site.'

'How about Abingers Pleasure Parlour?'

There was a stifled laugh. Nancy didn't want to hear more and tried to close her ears. The young men, whoever they were, were finding enjoyment in stripping some poor woman of her dignity.

'Which department does she work in?'

'Fine Art, I think. Fancy your luck?'

Nancy unblocked her ears.

'I don't think I've ever met her.'

'You wouldn't have. She's a peasant in the department. Second assistant or something. I guess the wages are pretty low. She probably needs to supplement them.'

'Even so, whoring is a bit beyond the pale, don't you think?'

'I'll say. But we might do worse for ourselves. Fancy a Nancy, eh?'

Nancy felt her fingers go numb, as though her blood had stopped circulating and her limbs had iced over. The tray she carried crashed from her hands, leaving a splatter of beef and gravy and apple pie across the tiled floor.

'Someone has to clean that up,' one of the servers behind the counter said, the woman's voice irate.

But Nancy didn't wait to hear more. She fled.

# Chapter Thirteen

Nancy ran from the basement, taking the stairs two at a time. Past Books on the ground floor, past the executive suite on the first, Fine Art on the second and a series of offices on the third, including her own. Then into the attics that flowed one into another, filling the very top floor of the building, and used by Abingers to store unwanted objects or items sent well ahead of their sale date. She crept from one to the other until, reaching the darkest corner she could find, she crouched down, folding into herself, her breath coming in rough gasps. At first, she felt nothing, her limbs numb, but gradually as the blood began to flow, her entire body was convulsed by pain.

Those men. Nancy didn't know them, but they knew her. No, they didn't know her, but they were happy to spread rumours about her, far and wide. Filthy rumours. It was then that she recalled the whispers she'd hardly been conscious of, the sly glances she'd dismissed as unimportant. They had been about her. Her name had been bandied throughout the auction house in the most dreadful fashion—and for how long?

It was then she began to cry, huge wracking sobs, tearing through her. She'd been attacked in the street, nearly lost her home, and now faced losing her job. The career she'd had such hopes for, was being taken from her. She would have to leave Abingers. She couldn't face the shame. Leave and find another job. But where?

A hand closed over hers and she looked up, her face wet with tears. It was Leo Tremayne.

'I was in the queue,' he said. 'I saw what happened. What upset you so much?'

'I can't tell you.' Her voice choked.

He knelt down, the small space beside her only just accommodating his tall figure. 'You can, Nancy. If you try.'

She blew her nose and tried to dap at her wet face.

'Here, take this. It's clean.'

'Thank you,' she said in a whisper. Mopping her cheeks with Leo's white linen handkerchief, she tried to speak. 'It was the men behind me,' she began.

'Yes?'

'They said something about a girl working at Abingers. That she was… that she wasn't what she should be. Only they didn't say it in those words,' she finished in a hardly audible voice.

'I'm sure they didn't,' Leo said grimly. 'And…'

'They were talking about me, Professor Tremayne,' she burst out. 'How could they?'

'Leo,' he reminded her gently. 'But why would they do such a thing?'

'You don't believe me? You think they're telling the truth?'

Leo took hold of her hand again. 'Of course I don't. But I want to know how it comes about that they were talking of you in that fashion. Where did they hear such a disgusting rumour in order to spread it? I take it, you don't know these fellows personally?'

Nancy shook her head. 'I've no idea how it started. Looking back, I suppose it's true that people have behaved a bit strangely towards me lately. I didn't really notice, though. I must have been sort of aware, but I didn't think much about it.'

'Why would you?

'And then those men…' She gulped back fresh tears and couldn't go on.

'Leave it with me.' Leo straightened up. 'I'll find out what's been going on. Discover the truth.' He looked down at her. 'Stay here if you like. Better still, go home and I'll explain to Mr Harker.'

'I can't do that.' Home didn't even feel like home anymore, she realised.

'Then I'll be back as soon as I can.'

And he was, an hour later, just as Nancy had decided that she couldn't hide away a minute longer.

'Sorry it's taken a while.' Leo dropped to the floor, folding himself almost double to sit beside her. 'I've been very thorough! Talked to a lot of people and I believe I've traced the culprit,' he said.

Nancy started forward. 'There's a culprit? Who?'

'A girl called Brenda Layton. She's one of the receptionists. You must know her.'

'Brenda! Are you sure?'

'As sure as I can be. I must have asked a dozen people if they'd heard the rumour and, if so, where had it come from? Several didn't want to say but out of those that did, one name came up repeatedly. And it was Brenda Layton's.'

Nancy felt her heart crumple. It was bad enough to know this horrible rumour was circulating Abingers, but to realise that one person—and that person a woman—had deliberately set out to slander her was wretched.

'I know Brenda doesn't particularly like me,' she said slowly, 'but why would she do such a spiteful thing? It could have had me dismissed.'

'I reckon that was probably the aim. She didn't come up with the idea herself, you know, though she seems to have adopted it with vigour.'

'So whose idea was it? Did you discover that as well?' Even as Nancy asked the question, she knew she could probably spell out the name.

'Your erstwhile fiancé. But I imagine you've guessed that. Apparently, he knows Brenda well.'

'He met her at the Christmas party and spent a lot of time talking to her,' Nancy said dully.

'It seems he's spent even more time lately. The rumour was his suggestion, and Miss Layton was enthusiastic. He'd get revenge on you and she'd get you dismissed or demoted. Either way, you suffered.'

'But why?' Nancy sounded despairing. 'Brenda doesn't like me, okay, but to do that…'

'Jealousy would be my guess.'

'Jealousy? What on earth is she jealous of? I'm a second assistant here and likely to stay one.'

'You're also a beautiful girl.' Nancy felt Leo's eyes rest on her for a moment, but then he said quickly, 'and even as a second assistant you work with important people. In Miss Layton's view, at least. That's more than she does as a receptionist.'

There was a long silence until Nancy said, 'How do you know about Philip's involvement?' It had occurred to her suddenly that he must have talked to Brenda.

'I've had words with Miss Layton,' he confirmed. 'About the evils of lying and lying to hurt others in particular. And I asked to see the Managing Director. I thought he should know what's been going on. I doubt Miss Layton will be staying at Abingers.'

Nancy sat up straight. 'I don't want her to lose *her* job.'

'Then you're far more forgiving than I am. At the moment, the MD is giving her the biggest dressing-down of her life. If she's lucky, she'll survive. Either way, I'm pretty sure she won't bother you again.'

'Thank you. Thank you so much…Leo,' she said. 'Now there's just the rest of the staff to face.' She got to her feet. 'I should be brave and go down.'

'The MD will be sending a letter to every employee, warning them of listening to and spreading malicious rumours. You might find that in the next few days everyone will be very friendly. Now how about that hot drink?'

*

Nancy sat in the café around the corner from Abingers. Mr Harker had readily agreed to Leo's suggestion that Miss Nicholson enjoy a short break away from the building. Mr Harker hadn't heard the gossip himself, he said, he was far too busy to fill his head with tittle tattle, but he was appalled to learn that Nancy had been the target of such vile abuse. Miss Layton would be on his radar from now on. Let that young woman step out of line for one moment and he would swoop.

Nancy sipped the hot tea and gave her companion a watery smile. 'Thank you again. I don't deserve that you've taken so much trouble.'

Leo looked at her for a moment. 'Why do you say that? You are a lovely young woman, bright, ambitious. It seems to me that you deserve a great deal more than any trouble I've taken.'

'That's very nice of you, but you must be so busy and I've wasted a huge amount of your time.'

'I'm not so busy that I can't help a damsel in distress!'

'But the tea—you didn't have to bring me here.'

'You needed to get out of Abingers. So did I, for that matter. I've an appointment at the travel agents in precisely,' he looked at his wrist-watch, 'one hour's time. My assistant is busy with other work, and I promised I'd be the one to collect the tickets. Till then, you're helping me pass the time very pleasantly.'

He *was* nice, Nancy thought. 'Are you going anywhere special?' she dared to ask.

'Special as in abroad?'

'That's special to me.'

'I've planned a visit to Madrid, but that's more like a holiday. Then a few days in New York and in September a conference in Venice.'

'I'd love to go to Venice.'

'You must, Nancy. It's a magical city and I'm sure you'd love it. I'm there to work, but it will still be very enjoyable.'

'What kind of conference is it?'

'In a nutshell, how to save Venice and its treasures from future flooding.'

'Is there much danger of that?'

Leo spread his hands. 'The city has always had a problem with water chipping away at its foundations, but the situation is becoming progressively worse. The conference is hoping to put together a programme—and the finance—to plan for the future. I'm setting up an Art Fund here for that very reason and I'll be using the conference to scout for sponsors.'

He went on talking, telling her who would be attending the conference, what he hoped to achieve by setting up the Art Fund, how much money needed donating, until his tea grew cold and he had to ask the waitress for another pot. Nancy felt herself lifted by his optimism, his sheer enthusiasm. Of late, both had been sorely lacking in her life.

As they were leaving the café, Leo took a card from his wallet and scribbled something on the back. 'My business number is printed here,' he pointed to the glossy side of the card. 'If you ring that, you'll get Archie Jago, my assistant. I've written my private number on the other side. If you need me, Nancy, don't hesitate to ring.'

She was astonished.

'You never know, you might want help,' he said, seeing her face. 'So call me. Please.'

Nancy squirrelled the card away in her handbag. 'Thank you for being so thoughtful,' she said with real gratitude.

'Don't thank me. I'm not being entirely altruistic. I like you, Nancy. A lot.'

It was another shock. If anything, Leo Tremayne's attitude to her had been fatherly. He hadn't shown the slightest sign of being attracted to her as a woman, but it seemed she'd been blind. She wished, though, that he hadn't said that. She liked him a good deal, but not in that way. He was an interesting man, hugely professional, and she enjoyed talking to him. But she felt no great attraction.

Friendship was best. She had learned that to her cost. She had fallen for Philip, been besotted by him, and it was difficult now to understand why. She had only to look at the road their relationship had travelled to realise how dangerous attraction could be.

# Chapter Fourteen

The past week had been Nancy's happiest for a considerable time. There had been no more silent phone calls and no further confrontations. She had walked home from the bus stop, visited the library, shopped at the corner store, unmolested. At work, her colleagues had gone out of their way to be friendly—even Brenda Layton had apologised, if grudgingly.

And this had been another good day. Free from the endless tension of wondering what disaster she'd face next, Nancy had thrown herself into her work, making sure there were no more mistakes. This morning, Mr Harker had given her the job of persuading a new client that Abingers was exactly the right auction house for a man wishing to sell his valuable antiques. She had been flattered and excited, but nervous, too. It was rare she was entrusted with that level of responsibility. But afterwards she thought she had done a good job, and when Mr Harker relayed the news later that day that the man was now their customer, Nancy felt an inner glow that had long been absent.

'Well done, Miss Nicholson,' he said, vigorously pumping her hand up and down. 'I can see I'll have to ask you to conduct these meetings more often.'

Several members of staff had planned a group visit that

evening and invited Nancy to come with them. She'd been doubtful but they'd insisted and, in the end, she had said yes, even rushing to Dickins & Jones in her lunchtime to buy a special dress, only to find the outing was to a local pub and everyone would still be in their work clothes. She was tired after what had been an exhausting day and would have preferred to go directly home, but it was important to build bridges and this was a chance.

At six o'clock, she tidied her desk and slipped on her jacket. Her fellow workers were waiting in the foyer and, as a group, they set off to stroll the short distance to the *Grapes of Wrath*. Philip had often suggested visiting one pub or another and Nancy had been happy to accompany him, though she rarely drank more than a fruit squash.

But this evening her colleagues intended that she enjoy herself and were keen to ply her with offers of alcohol. If she'd accepted only half of them, she would soon have been unable to stand. Instead, she took a single gin and drank it very slowly, feeling relaxed in their company, freed from the disgusting slur she'd suffered. Even the two men, whom she'd overheard in the cafeteria, made a point of coming up to her and sheepishly offering their apologies. For the first time in weeks, she found herself smiling without effort.

It had been a convivial evening, her companions generous in their sympathy and eager to make her feel better. But despite Nancy's pleasure at being part of the group, an hour or so of her colleagues' banter in the hot, stifling atmosphere of the *Grapes* was more than enough and she longed to leave for home. The chance came when one bright young man suggested they wander to the next pub, a few minutes away, where he said they could get a decent pie and chips.

'I hope you'll excuse me,' Nancy said. 'I've promised to have supper with a friend this evening.' It was only a white lie, she comforted herself.

There was a murmur of disappointment, but when the group tumbled out into the street, she was able to wave them a good-natured farewell. Tired but happy, she started on the journey home, looking forward to a peaceful few hours listening to the radio. She might just catch *The Archers*.

As soon as she opened the door to her room, Nancy knew that someone had been there. She'd wondered about it before—when she'd lost the sugar bowl, mislaid her shoes. But tonight, there was a definite feeling in the air, a cushion disturbed, a chair at a slight angle. She felt her breath catch slightly. Had *he* been here? She had never retrieved the keys she had given him in case of an emergency.

But she was letting fear rule her again, and she mustn't. Shutting the door softly behind her, she almost tip-toed across the sitting area and into the tiny kitchenette. Gazing around, Nancy could detect no change. Perhaps it was the unaccustomed alcohol sharpening her senses. More likely, her nerves hadn't quite settled and were still tense enough for fear to return in an instant. Deliberately, she loosened her shoulders and breathed deeply. She had to get over this, put it behind her.

She slipped off the light jacket she was wearing and walked towards the bedroom, in effect little more than an extension of the main room. Something made her pause in the archway. In the faint light trickling from the sitting room, she saw a small heap on the mat by her bedside. Nancy peered down at it, heart beating loud in her ears. Her blue silk dress, the most expensive frock she'd ever owned, had been cut into tiny, jagged pieces. She knelt on the mat and, for several minutes, cradled in her hands what was left of the once elegant garment. Then straightened abruptly and looked wildly around. What else?

By now, she knew what Philip was capable of. There was bound to be more. Her gaze fell on the top drawer of her chest. It was hanging open and, as her eyes focussed, she became aware of pieces of underwear, torn to shreds, spilling from the drawer and strewn in a circle around her bed.

Her tormentor was back. He'd given up accosting her, abandoned the anonymous phone calls, no doubt fearing discovery, and now he was violating her home. Destroying her most intimate possessions. She couldn't let him win. With huge effort, she tried to still a pulse that was tumultuous. Tried to breathe normally.

But then, raising her eyes to the wall above the bed, she saw scrawled in bright red lipstick: *Jezebel.*

She felt herself shivering violently, unable to stop the tremors. Her ears rang, her eyes hurt with the tears she was unable to shed. She felt angry and sick and terrified. She had to get away, away from this. Rushing from the room, she tumbled down the stairs and out onto the pavement, running blindly through the streets. A summer evening, the air warm, flies buzzing lazily, couples strolling hand in hand, and Nancy running as though from life itself.

Without realising, she had reached Paddington Station. A line of taxis barred her way, bringing her to a sudden halt. Her chest was heaving, and she could barely breathe.

'Want a taxi, dahlin?' one of the drivers asked.

Nancy shook her head and walked past into the station. The departures board loomed in front of her and she looked blankly up at it, numbers and places and times jiggling before her eyes. If only she could take one of those waiting trains and simply disappear. But where to? She had nowhere to go. Her parents wanted nothing more to do with her. Could she go to Rose? She had never sent the letter, yet she knew her friend would help. But Rose had a husband and young children and Nancy couldn't involve her in a nightmare that was hers alone.

Her legs were still trembling, feeling no more substantial than rags. Hopelessly, she looked around at the scurrying people, the banks of suitcases, the porters and their trolleys darting here and there. Through the thick steam of a departing engine, her eye was caught by the bright red of a telephone box. It was at the entrance to one of the platforms and Nancy found herself gravitating towards it. In the dim light of the box, she fumbled in her pocket for change. One penny, two, three.

Leo's card was in her other pocket—she had taken to carrying it with her—and her fingers were dialling his number. She heard the bell echoing through an empty house. It rang for a long time and no one answered. Holding the receiver so tightly that her finger bones almost cracked, she gradually came to her senses. What was she doing? Why was she ringing a man she hardly knew? She was being driven insane, that was why. Leo couldn't help her, and it was unfair to ask him. Nancy put the telephone down and pushed open the heavy metal door.

It closed slowly behind her and she stood, gazing abjectly at the bustling crowd passing by. Taxis offloaded their passengers, people rushed for trains, searching for tickets as they ran. Everyone hurrying. Everyone with a purpose. Then the telephone rang in the call box behind her, and went on ringing. It was seconds before she realised it could possibly be for her. There was only one way to find out and she heaved the door open again.

'Nancy? Is that you?' It was Leo, and somehow he'd known the missed call had been from her.

'Yes,' she said in a whisper. 'I'm in trouble, Leo. My room, someone…' She couldn't finish.

'Are you at your flat now?'

'No, Paddington,' she managed to say.

'The station?'

'Yes. Platform three…There's a phone box…'

'Stay there. I'll be with you in ten minutes.'

\*

Leo Tremayne took her back to his house in Cavendish Street. Or at least the man who drove them did.

'Archie Jago,' Leo introduced him. 'My assistant.'

The man had amazingly blue eyes and stared at her in what Nancy felt was a silent interrogation. He was weighing her up, she was certain, wondering why his employer had seemingly taken leave of his senses and collected this stray woman from a station platform.

The Marylebone townhouse that Leo owned was palatial, to Nancy at least, used as she was to the Riversley cottages and her parents' modest bungalow. Leo led her down to the spacious basement kitchen — his assistant had disappeared as soon as they'd walked through the front door — and made tea for them both. Then carrying a loaded tray, he ushered her up the stairs to the first-floor drawing room. From here, there was a grand view of the elegant road beyond, a symphony of black railings and white doorsteps.

Nancy took the cup Leo offered her and tried to relax, settling herself back into the depths of the armchair.

It was several minutes before he spoke. 'Can you tell me why you're so upset, Nancy? Though you don't have to, if you don't want to.'

She told him. About the invasion of her room, the ruined dress, the wrecked underwear, but made no mention of the words scrawled across her bedroom wall. That was too difficult to say.

'So this man is now getting into your flat,' Leo said. He sounded puzzled. 'Do you leave the door unlocked?'

'Philip has a key, or rather keys. There's a lock on the front door as well. I wanted him to have them when…' She trailed off.

'No point in asking for them back, I suppose?'

Nancy shook her head, feeling immensely weary.

'Then you must change the locks. Both of them.'

That would involve Mrs Minns. It would mean she would have to confess she was being harassed by a half-crazed man, and Mrs Minns needed no further excuse to ask her to leave.

Her hesitation was obvious. Leo leaned across and took her hands in a firm grasp. 'You must, Nancy. Do it tomorrow. It will put a stop to all of this. I can call a locksmith for you, or Archie can. And no need to worry about the bill.'

She shook her head.

'Why do you shake your head? It will work, I promise.'

'If I change the locks, Philip will find some other way to torment me. I thought he'd lost interest in this horrible game he's playing, but I know now that he's not giving up.'

Leo put his teacup down and sat back in the deep-cushioned armchair. 'You should have gone to the police ages ago,' he said mildly.

'They wouldn't have been interested.'

'They will now. The man is guilty of breaking and entering. That's a criminal act.'

Nancy shook her head again. 'He'll tell them I gave him a key, which I did, and so it's not breaking and entering.'

Leo leaned forward suddenly. 'And cutting up your clothes? That isn't a crime?'

'You don't know, Philip. He has a silver tongue. He'll say it was simply a lovers' tiff and, even if I say otherwise, it will be him the police believe. They will always take a man's word.

I'll be considered a hysterical woman.' She gave a sad smile.

'If you get the locks changed tomorrow, and he tries to do it again, it *will* be breaking and entering. He won't be able to wriggle out of that.'

Leo was so certain and so earnest that Nancy found herself agreeing, though she hadn't the money for two expensive new locks. And she'd no intention of accepting her host's offer.

'I'll do it tomorrow, I promise.'

'I'll sleep a lot easier knowing that.' He picked up the teapot. 'Can you drink another cup?'

## Chapter Fifteen

But perhaps changing the locks could wait for a day, Nancy said to herself, when she was once more back at Chilworth Road. Now that Philip had made his point—that he could walk in and out of her home without hindrance, and take, destroy, whatever he wanted—he probably wouldn't return. He'd be keen to think of another way of hurting her. And if he should decide to pay another visit, it wouldn't be soon. He'd let her fret for a few days, a few weeks even, leaving her nervous and agitated and fearful of when he'd be back. That would suit him admirably.

Tomorrow would be extremely busy, with little time to do anything but work. Nancy had been asked to help with the special display that Abingers was hosting to celebrate its founding and subsequent success. It was an illustrious history, begun in the eighteenth century, and gradually built on by generations of the Abinger family. Today, it was a modern firm, but its past as a confidante of princes from all over Europe and, more recently, business tycoons from the United States and Asia, made fascinating viewing.

Nancy's role was to staff the reception desk set up for the opening day. She was to register invited guests and ensure they were given a souvenir brochure and their own carefully chosen present, individually labelled. She had the caterers to oversee as well, checking that the right quantities of the right food had been delivered and were served at the right time. The day would be a challenge, but she was excited to be part of it.

It would leave no time, though, to contact a locksmith, but the following day was a Saturday and she wasn't down to work this weekend. She'd be free to call at the locksmith's then. It wouldn't hurt to hold fire for such a short time. The locksmith would be open until midday, and she'd make sure she arrived early with the request that he visit Chilworth Road once he'd closed the shop. She would order just the one lock, she decided, the one for her room, and cross her fingers it would prove sufficient—she couldn't face telling Mrs Minns that the front door lock should be changed, too. But even buying one lock, Nancy had no idea how she was to afford it. Perhaps, if she explained her predicament, the man would take a deposit and allow her to pay a weekly sum.

Meanwhile, before she slept tonight, she had a wall to clean. Until *Jezebel* was scrubbed clear away, the room would not feel home. Hot, soapy water at least blurred the image, but a great deal more effort was needed than a quick wash. It took an hour of scrubbing with a hard brush before she'd erased the last trace of red, though left behind was a ring of bare plaster. It was as well that she'd planned to repaint—but that would have to wait. Exhausted by the disaster her life had turned into, Nancy was feeling every one of her twenty-seven years.

*

She was at work by eight o'clock the next morning, to make sure the reception desk was correctly set up. The exhibition was planned to be a weekly event for the next month or so, but the opening day was particularly important. Abingers' management had invited a number of famous guests and all of them would expect special treatment.

For the last week or so Nancy had been knee-deep in arrangements, meticulously checking every last detail to ensure the event went without a hiccup, and was relieved when, by lunchtime, she felt able to pronounce the morning a success. There had been no complaints from the wealthy clientele—the opposite, in fact—and most had now left, bestowing a benevolent smile on her as they walked through the foyer.

Even the Managing Director, escorting one of their most prestigious clients, bent his head graciously and said, 'Wonderfully organised, Miss...' He peered at her name badge...Miss Nicholson.'

It was a long day. Even after Abingers had closed its doors, Nancy was still working, responsible for packing every item, every illustration and display board, safely away until the following week, when the exhibition would be open to the general public. Next Friday was likely to see more of a hubbub, but that was seven days away and she needn't think of it now. She had a weekend to enjoy.

On the way home, she bought herself fish and chips from the shopping parade near the bus stop. She shouldn't have done it, not with the expense of the locksmith to meet, but there had been a hint from Mr Harker that a modest bonus might be paid for the additional work she'd undertaken. And even if that didn't transpire, Nancy reckoned she deserved this simple treat.

The newspaper-wrapped fish and chips warmed her hands and smelt mouth-watering. She would make herself a large pot of tea, she decided, find the salt and vinegar, and sit down to a really good meal. Better still, when she opened the front door, Mrs Minns had her new television on very loudly and hadn't heard her come in—there would be no complaints of whatever was bothering her landlady this week. The television had been a godsend. The screen was a mere nine inches wide, but it kept Mrs Minns entranced for hours, and while she was entranced, she wasn't berating her lodgers.

But before Nancy reached the final flight of stairs that led to her room, she knew there was something wrong. He couldn't have come back, he simply couldn't. But there was something, something prickling in the air, some sense of disturbance washing down the staircase to greet her. She felt her breath stall for a moment, then clutching tightly to her parcel, she walked up the bare wooden steps, turned the corner and faced the door of her bed-sitting room. Except there was no door. Not to speak of. Two shattered pieces of wood hung from their hinges, smaller shards scattered across the landing.

She braced herself and walked into the kitchenette. A scene of devastation hit her. Every cupboard door hung open, every shelf had been swept clean of crockery, and broken glass crunched beneath her feet. The larder cupboard stood open, and she saw that food had been pulled out and whatever could be smeared—butter, sauce, a bowl of soup—had been splashed across the painted walls. Her entire kitchen had been trashed.

As if in slow motion, she dropped her parcel onto the kitchen table. The table at least had remained unbroken, but the rest was utterly destroyed. Edging past and into the sitting space, her eyes filled with tears and her heart hurt so badly she thought it might be torn from her body. The sofa she'd spent over a year saving for, had been ripped from top to bottom, the stuffing strewed liberally across the trampled mat.

It wasn't just her heart that hurt. Every limb was hurting.

But she forced herself to walk through the archway to the bedroom. Her bed—the pillows, the white counterpane—were still intact. She felt a bubble of relief. But there was something in the middle of the bed. A black shape. Nancy stood and stared, shuffling forward, unable to process what she was seeing. A dead crow, its beautiful black feathers already dulled, lay in a pool of red blood.

She heard a faint scream from somewhere far off. It was her. She was the one screaming. Galvanised, she turned and ran for the doorway, only to be brought up sharply by the figure of a man. She raised her fists, punching at him again and again, sobbing louder with every punch.

'Nancy,' a voice said urgently. 'It's me. Leo.'

## *Chapter Sixteen*

Nancy's hands were arrested mid-air and she looked at him, dazed and unseeing.

'It's Leo Tremayne,' he repeated. 'I need to get you out of here, Nancy. I've a cab waiting.'

Mutely, she allowed herself to be helped down the stairs, through the open front door and into the taxi.

'Archie—my assistant—has the car,' Leo explained. 'He's gone to Cornwall for a few days to see his folks. Hence the taxi.'

Nancy barely registered the fact, leaning back against the worn leather seat and closing her eyes. Her life was in ruins. She had been cut adrift from everything meaningful, and there was no fight left in her.

'You'll come through this,' Leo assured her, holding her hand until the taxi pulled up in front of the Cavendish Street house. 'I asked Mrs Brindley to make up an extra bed before she left. She's my housekeeper. She doesn't live in—I'm the only one here this evening.'

Once he'd paid the cabbie, Leo helped her up the front steps and into the house. 'This way,' he said, guiding her towards the stairs.

Nancy, still dazed, followed in his footsteps, pausing in the doorway of a beautifully appointed bedroom. 'How did you know?' she asked faintly.

'Know you'd come here? I didn't. But you were very distressed yesterday, and I thought it was possible you might be again. Always be prepared! The room is all right, I hope?'

'It's lovely.' The words were inadequate, but Nancy was still reeling.

'I'll let you settle in. There's a bathroom next door. All yours. When you feel ready, come downstairs and have something to eat. Mrs B will have prepared a meal for sure.'

Feeling awkward, Nancy said quietly, 'I don't have anything with me—night stuff, I mean.'

'There's toothpaste and soap in the bathroom. Towels as well. But I can only offer you pyjamas for tonight. There's a spare pair in the top drawer of the chest. I'll go back to Chilworth Road tomorrow and get your landlady to pack a bag for you.'

When he'd gone, Nancy slumped down on the bed and sat for a long while, trying to accept what had happened, trying to find some comfort in the luxury of this beautiful room. Her surroundings were certainly soothing, the walls pale grey and the long voile curtains a light cream. A deep button-backed chair in red velvet echoed the glowing colours of the Indian-inspired counterpane she'd creased so badly, and a vase of poppies sang the same tune from a dainty dressing table. It was an elegant and extremely comfortable retreat, Nancy thought, her feet sinking into thick carpet. But it wasn't where she should be.

She would have to be brave. She couldn't let Leo face Mrs Minns tomorrow. She would stay here tonight, grateful for the safe haven, and gird herself to face the terror of Chilworth Road in the morning. Would Mrs Minns have found her way to the top floor by now and discovered the appalling damage? Nancy would be made to pay for it, but how? Philip March had destroyed nearly everything she owned. How was she even to begin repaying the landlady?

She washed her face and brushed her hair and tried to smooth her clothes into some kind of order. Leo was waiting for her at the foot of the stairs and led the way down a second flight to the kitchen she'd seen only yesterday.

Supper was the last thing she wanted, but Mrs Brindley was an excellent cook and Nancy discovered more of an appetite than she'd expected. It was when she remembered the parcel of fish and chips, lying forlorn and cold on the Chilworth Road table, that her face shadowed.

'I didn't go into your room,' Leo said quietly, looking across at her, 'but what exactly did that evil man do?'

When she told him, he moved around the table and took hold of both her hands, crouching down beside her. 'You're not to worry, Nancy. Your landlady will be paid for every bit of damage. And for a thorough clean. If you want to stay there, I'll make sure it's a fit place for you to live in.'

Nancy withdrew her hands in a slight panic. 'You can't do that. I can't let you spend your money. It wouldn't be right.'

'You can and you will. I have more than enough for my own needs. You're in deep trouble. Let me help you. If it makes you feel better, call it a loan.'

'A loan I'll never be able to repay. At least not for years.'

'Then let it take years. I'm hoping, though, that you won't want to go back to Chilworth Road.'

'I'll have to, Leo.' She paused. 'To be honest, it's all I can afford.'

He nodded and straightened up. 'Maybe we can think of another solution.'

Nancy couldn't think what that might be, but a sudden thought had her put Leo's words aside. 'Why did you come to Chilworth Road this evening?' She'd been too dazed to consider it before.

'I was uneasy—after yesterday. Archie went off to Cornwall this morning, Mrs Brindley left about five, and I had the whole evening free. I thought I'd drop by and see if everything was okay with you.'

'But you walked into the house. How did that happen? The front door is always locked.'

'Not tonight, it wasn't. I was walking up the front path when the door opened and a chap came out. I'm pretty sure it wasn't your villain. He said a polite good evening and sauntered off whistling.'

'That would be Mrs Minns' other lodger. He must have been at work when my room was being destroyed. But he always goes to the pub on Friday evening—to play darts, I think he told me once.'

'A bit of luck then,' Leo said, piling their dirty plates into the sink. 'Now how about watching television for a while? There's a new series just started. Mrs Brindley was talking about it. No idea whether we'll like it or not, but it's a lazy way to spend an hour and maybe the right thing tonight.'

*Dixon of Dock Green* might have been an excellent programme, but only a short while into it, Nancy dropped off to sleep. The chair's deep cushions, the slight breeze coming through the open window, the soporific effect of the changing screen, and her sheer exhaustion sent her into such a heavy doze that Leo had to half carry her up the stairs to her room.

'Can you manage?' he asked anxiously, steering her through the doorway. 'I should have asked Mrs Brindley to stay on.'

'How could you have known I'd be here? I'm fine, Leo. Really. I can get myself to bed. I'm sorry I'm such a poor guest.'

Leo bent and kissed her on the cheek. 'You're a perfect

guest, Nancy. And one who's going to sleep very, very well.'

*

Despite a troubled mind, Nancy did. At least for a while, almost immediately falling back into a deep sleep. But several hours later, she was awake. Suddenly. Her throat was sore, her mouth dry and sweat was pouring off her. There had been a noise, she was sure. A scream?

'Nancy? Are you all right?'

Leo stood in the doorway, his figure silhouetted against the light streaming from the landing.

'I don't know,' she stammered, trying to pull herself upright.

'You screamed out.'

'Did I?' Her head felt groggy and her limbs seemed to have lost any strength. 'I must have had a nightmare. Yes, that was it… a nightmare. I'm sorry.'

He walked further into the room. 'It's hardly surprising. You've just endured a dreadful experience.' She could see the worry in his face. 'How about some tea? Could you drink a cup?'

Nancy felt her tongue stick and her mouth like ash. 'I'd love one, but—'

'Stay in bed. I'll be back.'

Within ten minutes, he was.

'Here. I found some mugs—easier to manage in bed.' He handed Nancy her tea and carried his own over to the red velvet chair. 'I know tea is supposed to invigorate, but I reckon it can soothe as well,' he said, taking a sip.

'I'm sure it will,' she said gratefully. 'I'm so sorry to wake you like this.' She tried a limp smile.

Leo wagged his finger. 'Stop saying sorry. After what you've been through, you're entitled to a nightmare or two.'

They finished their tea in silence. Leo collected the empty mugs, then stood looking down at Nancy's bed.

'Before I go, let me straighten those bedclothes. It looks as though you've been fighting the next world war.'

'You don't need —' she began, but he was already smoothing out the Indian counterpane and tucking in bedsheets that were hanging loose.

'Do you think you'll be okay, now?'

'I'm sure I will. And thank you.'

'Best time of the night to sleep — a few hours before dawn. But if you can't, if you feel bad, you must call me. I'm just along the landing.'

'You're very kind,' she murmured, snuggling down between the covers.

## Chapter Seventeen

The tea was as soothing as Leo had predicted and Nancy slept almost immediately, and went on sleeping until past eight o' clock in the morning. A dreamy glance at the small, brass clock had her almost jumping from the bed and stumbling to the door. Opening it a few inches, she listened for sounds of life, but the house was silent. Had Leo gone to Chilworth Road as he'd said he would? She scolded herself for oversleeping; she should have been the one to face Mrs Minns' wrath.

After washing and dressing in a hurry, she arrived in the kitchen as Mrs Brindley—Nancy presumed she must be the housekeeper—walked through the door. The woman stared, a severe expression on her face.

'I stayed the night,' Nancy said awkwardly. Then realising what that must sound like, added hastily, 'Professor Tremayne very kindly put me up. There was an… an accident… at my flat.'

Mrs Brindley came fully into the kitchen and dropped her basket onto the table. 'And where is the professor?' Her tone was tart.

'I'm not sure.' Nancy faltered, feeling more of an intruder than ever.

The housekeeper gave a snort, but whatever she was about

to say was cut thankfully short by the sound of the front door opening and footsteps on the stairs.

Leo smiled broadly at the two women. 'You've met. Excellent. Good morning to you both. Nancy—did you get to sleep? Have you had breakfast?'

She smiled back at him. 'Yes to the first question, and no to the second.'

'Then we must do something about it. Mrs B, be a dear and rustle up some breakfast for us both. I've had nothing this morning and I'm starving.'

In a short while Mrs Brindley, lips pursed, was laying out eggs, toast and coffee in a room that Nancy had not so far encountered. She supposed you would call it a formal dining room and suspected the housekeeper hadn't wanted them cluttering up the kitchen. This room occupied a relatively modest space but, as with everything in the townhouse, it spoke elegance. Pale cream walls, pale grey carpet and drapes of deep blue velvet.

'Did you go to Chilworth Road?' Nancy asked, once they'd begun on the toast. Despite her nervousness, she could wait no longer to discover what Leo had been up to this morning.

'I did, and I have to tell you that your landlady is not a happy woman. A bit happier, though, once I opened my wallet.' He grinned.

'She's discovered the damage?'

'Very definitely! Last night, I believe. She must have been out when it happened because she heard nothing, but the lodger on the floor below, the chap I passed at the front door, decided to call on you when he got back from the pub. Some story about wanting to make coffee but having run out of sugar.'

'He often does.'

'Well, when he came calling, he got something of a

surprise. He must have skipped downstairs that minute to inform Mrs Minns that the top floor of her house had been more or less demolished.'

Nancy held her breath. 'And Mrs Minns—you placated her?'

Leo pulled a face. 'Up to a point.'

'What does that mean?'

'It means she's not calling in the police, which in the circumstances is probably as well. She was persuaded to riffle through your wardrobe and pack a bag for you. I've left it in the hall. But it also means that once your room is put back together again, she plans to look for a new lodger.'

'She's evicting me?' A wave of desperation hit Nancy.

'Pretty much. She thinks you keep bad company. She mentioned strange phone calls in the night, and she thinks someone has been getting into the house when she's not around. Well, that was pretty obvious. So, all in all, my dear, you're not exactly welcome at number sixteen.'

Nancy couldn't speak. It was impossible to express the dread she felt. She would lose her job if she didn't return to work on Monday. But how was she to continue working without a roof over her head? Without a fixed address?

Her thoughts were racing, her mind unravelling. It would take for ever to find a place close enough to work that she could afford, and she had no one with whom she could stay temporarily. Rose was her only friend and she lived miles away. In any case, she'd decided days ago to keep Rose out of this trouble, and she wasn't going to change her mind.

Riversley? She would have to move back to Riversley. But that would mean losing her job. And there was no longer any kind of home for her there. How on earth was she to survive?

'I have an idea, Nancy.' Leo sounded reassuring and pulled up his chair to sit close to her. 'Only an idea, mind,' he went on. 'But I think it might solve a number of problems.'

She half turned to face him. 'What?' she asked eagerly.

He didn't reply immediately but shifted around in his seat. He seemed suddenly uncomfortable, but why? What on earth was he about to suggest?

'You might not like it,' he said at last, 'but I think it would work.'

'Yes, you said. But what is it?'

'Why don't you marry me?'

'What!' Nancy's eyes opened wide, her eyebrows shooting upwards.

He took hold of her hand; it lay cold in his warm grasp. 'I know it sounds crazy. But we know each other—a little. We've talked often and our work means we've a lot in common.' He gave her fingers a gentle squeeze. 'I liked you from the moment we met, and I think I'd make a decent husband. I'd make sure you have the best of everything. You would never have to live in a place like Chilworth Road again.'

Nancy withdrew her hand from his clasp. 'You're astonishing, Leo. And so kind. But you can't know what you're saying. Not really.' She was grappling with the enormity of what he'd suggested.

'Oh, but I do. I've been thinking about it for weeks. I've never mentioned to you how I feel—for very good reason. I'm a good deal older than you, my dear. Forty-five years old. And that matters. You're young, you're beautiful, you're talented. You could do a lot better. But I'd look after you, Nancy, you can be sure of that.'

'I'm flattered. Truly flattered. And utterly amazed that you'd make such an offer.' She wanted to hug him for his generosity, except that it would be entirely the wrong thing to do. 'But I can't marry you to solve my housing problem.'

'It wouldn't only be an answer to where you live, though,

would it? If you married me, I'd be your protector, your security. Once this March creature realises you're forever beyond his reach, he'll disappear. There would be little point in his continuing to harass you.'

Nancy was unsure Leo's argument was sound. If Philip had ever loved her, he certainly didn't now. What he wanted was power, not love. Power over her to exact his vengeance. Leo was speaking as though Philip March was a rational being, but he wasn't. It wasn't reason driving him. And if she were ever mad enough to accept this wonderful man's offer, she would not be telling March or anyone who knew him.

Leo moved his chair back and began gathering up the empty plates. 'Look, I've sprung it on you, but over the next few days, give it some thought. Please. I've a strong feeling, instinct if you like, that our life together would be good. I've lived a fair few years now, but I've never wanted to marry. You're the first woman I've met that I've wanted to be close to.'

It was an enormous compliment and she was touched by it.

He dropped a light kiss on the top of her head and made for the door, a loaded tray in his hands. 'I'll not be a moment. I'll shoot these down to the kitchen.' He paused in the doorway.

'I love you,' he said, before disappearing.

# Chapter Eighteen

The problem was that Nancy didn't love him. Not in the way Leo would want. Not in the way he deserved. She sank back into the chair, hands clutching the padded arm rests, trying to think what was best to do. She should leave immediately, she decided. Find another room, whatever or wherever it was. And find it today.

There was little point in looking locally; the rents in Marylebone would be far too high. She would need to go back to Paddington, visit the newsagent she knew and sift through the cards in his window. An unenviable task. First, though, she must tackle another just as daunting. She must telephone Abingers and try to explain her situation. Staff took it in turns to work Saturdays, but Mr Harker made sure he was always in.

When she went to find Leo again to ask if she could use the telephone, he brushed it aside. 'No need. I've spoken to Abingers myself.'

She gaped. 'When?'

'After my exciting visit to Chilworth Road. I got the cabbie to take me on to Abingers. I knew the MD would be in early — he had an appointment with me at nine.'

And…?' she asked, her teeth on edge.

'And it's fine. I explained—in general terms only—that

your accommodation was no longer habitable. I allowed him to think it was a gas explosion or some such thing. And that you needed time to find somewhere else to live.'

'And he was okay with that?' Nancy was amazed if that was the case.

'Absolutely. He understood perfectly.'

'And Mr Harker? He's my immediate superior.'

'Mr Harker will be told the problem and will expect you back as soon as you're ready. But not before!'

'You are a miracle worker, Leo.'

'On a very modest scale. Now, what do you intend to do with your day? Or need I ask?'

'I have to start searching. In Paddington, I think.'

'I hate the idea of your having to drag yourself from one room to another, but I'm hoping you'll give my suggestion some thought—it would make me very happy. And while you're thinking, how about contacting your parents? Maybe moving in with them for a few days?'

Nancy looked down at her feet. 'I don't speak to them,' she said very quietly.

'Really? Obviously, I don't know what's gone on, but don't you think this might be the right time to begin talking? Tell them what's been happening. They'd want to look after you, I'm sure.'

She shook her head vigorously. 'I've tried talking to them, but they refused to believe me. In their eyes, Philip March can do no wrong.'

He was silent for a moment, evidently thinking hard. 'How about I hire a car and drive down to Hampshire—it is Hampshire, isn't it? I could collect them and take them to Chilworth Road. They'd have to change their minds then.'

'No! I don't want them here. I don't want them to see the room.' Nancy felt tears start in her eyes.

'Why ever not?' Leo was clearly mystified.

'I'd be ashamed,' she muttered.

'Ashamed? But you have nothing whatever to be ashamed of.'

Nancy steeled herself to look directly into his eyes. 'I've always been a disappointment to my parents. And this is one more failure—probably the worst yet.'

Leo walked over to her and hugged her tight. For a moment, she allowed herself to nestle against him, but pulling away, she said, 'Time's getting on, Leo. I must go.'

'Do you want me to come with you? In case March is still roaming Paddington? I don't need to buckle down to work for a day or so. Archie won't be back for at least a week and I'm keen he's not faced with too much catching up when he returns. So… I'm at your disposal.'

'No,' she said hurriedly. 'You mustn't let me disturb you any more than I already have. I'm sure I won't meet Philip today. He'll be too busy celebrating his success.'

The last thing Nancy wanted was for Leo to see the kind of rooms she'd be offered. She was inured to the shabby accommodation her money could buy, but he would be appalled.

'You thought that before,' he warned. But then, as if sensing her discomfort, he said, 'If you're sure? I'll see you back here when you've had enough of traipsing London's streets.'

*

It proved a dismal day. A tense day, too, since despite Nancy's confident assertion that Philip March would be savouring his victory elsewhere, she remained wary: using caution when she rounded corners, taking note of people walking towards her, staying alert to other customers in the corner stores she visited.

Her search began at the newsagent nearest Chilworth Road, but in all she must have called on half a dozen businesses, including several corner shops and an agency that rented out apartments. She found nowhere she could make her home. Towards the end of the day, she was shown a pretty one-bedroomed flat in a neat terrace of houses, but the rent was almost double what she could afford and she was forced to turn it down. The few rooms that were available were available for a reason. All of them smaller and darker than Chilworth Road, and varying in degrees of shabbiness, one verging on the squalid.

'I'll try Notting Hill tomorrow,' Nancy said that evening, over another delicious meal. She'd had no alternative but to spend a second night in Cavendish Street, though she felt it unfair to Leo.

He made no comment, but his eyebrows rose in a silent question. The next two days were no different from the first, except that Nancy decided to note down any telephone numbers she found—she was still uneasy walking the streets alone—and, once back in Cavendish Street, diligently rang each one, only to find the room had gone or the rent originally quoted was now a good deal higher.

By her fourth evening, she was feeling truly desperate. After dinner, she sat with Leo in the sitting room, trying to read a book, but a few minutes later, she laid the volume aside.

'I think I might try going further afield tomorrow,' she said bravely. 'Belsize Park perhaps. There might be more choice there.'

'Is that wise? Your journey to work would be a good deal longer.'

She felt a jolt of exasperation and bit her lip. It wasn't Leo's fault, but he had no real understanding of the difficulties.

'Why not have tomorrow off?' he suggested. 'I was thinking we could venture out together.'

'Venture out?' she echoed.

'How about visiting the zoo?'

Her strained expression vanished and she laughed. 'I've never been.'

'Then tomorrow's the day. We can walk in Regent's Park afterwards. Have a cup of tea at the café there.'

It sounded infinitely preferable to trudging the streets of north London, and Nancy found herself agreeing, though she knew she should continue her dismal search. But if she were to spend the day with Leo, she had to be honest. He had asked her to think over his proposition—she couldn't really call it a proposal, though in essence that was what it was—and after several nights of tussling with her conscience, her mind was unchanged. If she could have said yes, it would have made her life blissfully easy: a beautiful house to live in, beautiful clothes to wear, foreign travel and, above all, safety. But she couldn't do it. Leo was too decent a man to deceive into thinking she could love him as a wife.

'About the...the suggestion...you made.'

He leaned forward from his chair. 'You've been thinking about it?'

'A lot. I like you enormously, Leo. I'm very fond of you,' she said as gently as she could. 'But I don't love you enough to marry. I would be doing you a grave injustice if I agreed to.'

'What if I don't mind?'

'Of course, you mind. Any man would. You deserve a woman who can properly love you. You haven't waited all these years to marry, to be palmed off with a flimsy semblance of it.'

'Love can grow, Nancy. Didn't your mother ever tell you?'

She couldn't imagine Ruth Nicholson ever voicing such a sentiment, but it was a familiar saying. It wasn't going to work here, though, Nancy was fairly sure. Leo was good looking, wealthy and at the top of his profession. He would be a 'catch' for any woman. But not for her. She respected his expertise and admired him enormously. He was a man with whom she could be friends, but not a man she wanted for a lover.

'Don't reject the idea completely,' he urged. 'Let the matter keep turning in your mind.' Had he sensed some hesitation in her, she wondered?

\*

The day was sultry, one of those days in late August when the freshness of summer has waned, but the sun still feels hot, even through low cloud. By the time they had strolled the short distance to Regent's Park, they were both sticky and uncomfortable. The zoo was another ten minutes' walk away and once inside, Nancy thought, they would feel even stickier.

'What do you say we just wander?' Leo asked.

'Perfect,' she agreed. 'I can visit the zoo another time.'

'With me, I hope.'

Nancy said nothing but took a silent vow. She must disentangle herself from Leo's life as quickly as possible; it was the kindest thing she could do. In the next day or so, she must take whatever room she could find. Soon he would journey to Venice and their separation would be complete.

'When do you leave for your conference?' she asked, as they sat in the café licking cones of vanilla ice cream.

'Early September. Next week, in fact.' Leo seemed surprised the date had come round so quickly. 'There's stuff to get ready still, but I'm more or less organised. I'll leave the finishing touches for Archie when he gets back.'

'He lives at Cavendish Street?'

Nancy thought it more than likely. She had seen him disappear up the stairs to a higher floor the night he had driven Leo to Paddington Station and brought her back to the house in tears.

'He has the top floor. It's a one person flat—bedroom, sitting room, kitchenette, and bathroom. The house is too big for a single man, and it's been handy having him living on site.'

Lucky Archie, she thought. His flat sounded heavenly, an oasis to a parched woman.

'Do you know where you're staying in Venice?' Nancy wanted him to keep talking. Wanted to keep the worries at bay, for one day at least.

'The conference is at the Cini library and is being organised by the great and good of Venice. They'll have booked us into a hotel. Not sure which one, but there'll be a mass of delegates to accommodate.'

'Putting on an event like that must be costly.'

'Very. But there are some wealthy individuals in the city, willing to put their hands in their pockets. A chap I knew at university, Dino di Maio, is funding a good deal of it. It gives him kudos, I guess, but he's a Venetian and has a deep loyalty to his birthplace. He wants it to survive.'

Leo crunched the last piece of his cone and wiped his hands on the paper napkin.

'Will you be speaking at the conference?' She felt a genuine interest.

'Much of my time will be spent fact-finding, but I've been given a slot on the programme. When I speak, I'll be trying to gather support for the Art Fund I mentioned. Keeping Venice and its treasures safe is going to take an awful lot of cash. I want to get as many commitments to the fund as I can. If I come away empty-handed, I'll be disappointed.'

'I'm sure that won't happen. You're so enthusiastic, you're bound to bring the money in!'

'Let's hope so!'

# Chapter Nineteen

The following day, Nancy returned early to Cavendish Street. She had set off in good heart that morning, travelling northwards to Swiss Cottage and Belsize Park, ready to brave unfamiliar streets and take whatever was on offer. In the event, not one room was available to view and by three in the afternoon, after countless enquiries, she decided it was pointless to continue. Her legs felt as leaden as her heart.

Walking through the front door of the Marylebone house, she found Leo had not yet returned. He had appointments for most of the day, she knew. But the frightening Mrs Brindley was still much in evidence. Nancy had kept out of the housekeeper's way as much as possible, but felt guilty seeing her at work when she had done nothing to earn her own bed and board.

'Can I help with the vegetables?' she asked, hovering in the kitchen doorway.

'Mr Leo pays me to look after the house,' the woman said stiffly.

'I realise that, but I hoped I might help a little.'

Mrs Brindley gave a loud sniff. 'If you're any good with flowers, you can arrange those.' She pointed to an enormous bouquet, still wrapped in the florist's cellophane and abandoned on the kitchen table. 'Another darn bunch—I'm sick of 'em. Why women with more money than sense have to send the professor flowers, just because he's put a good price on their wretched paintings, I dunno.'

'What do they send if he hasn't?' Nancy dared to ask.

Mrs Brindley glared at her, and she was quick to scoop up the flowers and take them into the small room off the kitchen. A kitchen off a kitchen, Nancy marvelled.

She found a tall, glass vase in one of the cupboards, and laying aside the envelope that contained the sender's card, did her best with the blooms—a stunning collection of roses, veronica, daisies and dragon snaps. She walked them up the stairs to the hall and was about to balance the card beside them, when an urge took hold of her to open the envelope. What kind of women sent Leo such gorgeous flowers?

*To my very own dear, Nancy,* she read. *To thank you for a wonderful few days—and hoping for many more. Leo.*

She dropped the card as though it were on fire. Leo had sent her flowers. He shouldn't be sending flowers, shouldn't be writing like this. As though they were together, a couple. She tucked the card in her pocket, not wanting Mrs Brindley to see it, and retreated to her bedroom. It seemed Leo was still intent on marrying her. Clearly, her refusal hadn't been forceful enough. It had allowed him to hope she would change her mind. And why was that? Because she was in two minds herself? Because, she thought bitterly, every day she stayed at Cavendish Street, sheltered and safe, made it more difficult to leave.

The front door slammed and she heard Leo's voice calling.

'Come and see, Nancy. I've a treat. Champagne. We must drink champagne.'

She walked slowly down the stairs to meet him in the hall. He held a large bottle aloft.

'Why champagne? What's it for?'

'What is it for? For you, Nancy. And me. I see the flowers have arrived.' He looked down at the slightly askew arrangement.

'They have and thank you. They're beautiful. But you shouldn't have sent them. You shouldn't have bought champagne either.'

Mrs Brindley appeared at the top of the stairs that led up from the kitchen. 'The casserole is in the oven, Professor. There's pudding in the fridge.'

'Thank you, Mrs. B. See you in the morning.'

When the housekeeper had closed the front door behind her, Leo put the bottle down on the table and, taking both of Nancy's hands in his, began to waltz her up and down the hall in a wild dance.

'What are you doing?' She was laughing and out of breath. 'Stop, Leo. Or I'll be so dizzy, I'll end face down on the carpet.'

'The flowers and champagne are in honour of my dear guest, Nancy Nicholson.' He stopped waltzing and stood facing her, still holding her hands. 'In the hope that she'll make me the happiest man in England.'

'I can't, Leo. I really can't. Please believe me.'

He didn't move but stood looking down into her eyes. 'I think you can, Nancy.'

She felt immense discomfort. Surely, now, she had made her feelings as plain as she could. Yet Leo was ignoring her words, refusing to accept her decision. It had begun to feel a little as though he was trying to control her. Another man controlling her? Nancy gave herself an inner shake. It wasn't at all like that. Leo had been as kind as he possibly could be. She must tell him no again—and tell him again and again, if necessary. Eventually he was bound to accept it.

After supper that night, they settled in armchairs to watch the news on Leo's new television. When it was finished, he switched off the set, and came to stand beside her.

'The Fitzrovia Chapel has a cancellation.'

'I'm not sure I know the Fitzrovia Chapel.' His remark puzzled her.

'It's close by. A splendid wedding venue. Normally, you have to book months in advance, but I called in there today, and they just happen to have a cancellation. The day after tomorrow. What do you think?'

'Leo, I—'

'Don't say it. I know your objections, but I don't accept them. This—the friendship we have—is too good to abandon, and that's what will happen when you move out. Okay, you don't feel as deeply for me as I do for you. But it doesn't worry me. What worries me is losing you. I want to be with you forever. Can't you understand that?'

'But—'she began again.

'The thing is, Nancy, darling. I can call you darling? You've looked for days for somewhere to live and you haven't found anywhere you feel comfortable with. Anywhere you'll be safe from that maniac. You know I have to go to Venice in a very few days now? Naturally, I don't mind your staying here while I'm away, but it's not a long- term solution to your problem. We live in a censorious society and Mrs Brindley is already getting twitchy about the length of your stay. I think you'll have to find somewhere to live before I go.'

Nancy felt herself pale. She had known this was coming, had lectured herself that she had to leave as soon as possible. But now it was real, and the thought of abandoning this comfortable, safe house for whatever unknown terror lay ahead, was devastating.

'Or,' Leo said, 'you could marry me and come with me to the conference.'

'To Venice?' She tried not to think of a long-held dream

coming true.

'To Venice. To anywhere in the world. Why not throw your lot in with me? I promise I'd make it worth your while!'

She smiled at that. 'I know you would, Leo,' she said sadly. 'But I'd be short-changing you. I can't do it.'

'That's how you see it. I don't and if I don't, why should it matter to you? Say yes, Nancy.'

He pulled her up onto her feet and kissed her full on the lips. He had a nice mouth, she decided, warm lips and warm arms. She felt herself sink against him, her head on his chest. How wonderful no longer to struggle. No longer live so meanly. No longer worry that an unhinged man would destroy her possessions, her comforts, even her life. She was certain Philip would not stop at smashing things. He would want to smash her, too.

'Well?' Leo looked down at her and kissed her again. 'What's it to be?'

# Chapter Twenty

Leo continued to persuade and Nancy to listen. Later, she supposed it was only a matter of time before she succumbed to temptation. She found him an attractive man, liked him enormously, and was in awe of his professional expertise. Good marriages had been based on less, she was sure. And when she looked to a future alone, there were no paths she wanted to travel.

If only she could have seen ahead to a better paid job at Abingers—one that would allow her to rent safe accommodation, a decent apartment. Or friends who could offer her a home. Or parents willing to support her. But every path led to a dark, dead end. And now it was imperative that she leave the one piece of security she'd known in months.

Leo was putting pressure on her, though she couldn't blame him. He was right in saying that she couldn't stay at Cavendish Street indefinitely, and to stay here even for a short time while he was miles away would provoke gossip he didn't deserve. She would no longer be considered his guest but a kept woman. And he was using that as leverage to get what he wanted. She could say no, of course she could. But she wasn't going to. It was too easy to say yes.

The next day passed in a blur. A visit to the chapel in the morning and a brief  conversation with the churchman who would officiate. As Leo had said, Fitzrovia was an astonishingly beautiful church in which to marry. A vaulted, golden ceiling spread with stars, stained glass windows that glowed bright colour, and walls of marble, interwoven with intricate mosaics.

'I think you'll find our chapel a wonderful fusion of beauty and history,' the priest intoned.

'And don't let's forget the Gothic charm,' Leo put in, a wry smile lighting his face.

Nancy was silent, feeling overwhelmed by a space so very different to the chapel familiar to her from childhood. But she'd ceased almost to think, allowing herself to be carried unprotestingly on a wave that would deliver her to the altar.

They were halfway back on their walk home, when Leo stopped and gestured to a street running at right angles. 'If you take that road, you'll hit Oxford Street. Turn right at the bottom and Selfridges won't be far.'

She looked up at him, perplexed.

'Your wedding dress?' he suggested.

Why hadn't she thought of that? 'But Selfridges will be expensive,' she protested.

'And so it should be. I hope this is the first and last wedding dress you'll ever wear. You must buy some cotton frocks at the same time—for Venice—and a new silk dress to replace the one you lost. Anything, in fact, that you need for your wardrobe. Oh, and while you're in the store, have your hair done.'

'I don't think—' Nancy began.

'You don't need cash,' he said quickly. 'I have an account there. Just mention my name.'

He must have seen the panic in her eyes. But to use a shop account? It would be a novel experience. She kissed him on the cheek and ten minutes later was taking the escalator to

Selfridge's bridal department.

A few more minutes and she had a trio of black-suited saleswomen running backwards and forwards to find her the perfect wedding dress. They did it in double quick time. An ivory satin gown with a full skirt falling just below the knee, and a lace bodice cut front and back into a deep vee. It fitted to perfection and, when one of the frighteningly smart assistants produced oyster satin shoes and a matching flower to wear in her hair, Nancy knew she would look the best she could.

A tea dress in red silk followed and three cotton frocks of different designs. She had only meant to buy two but, in the end, hadn't been able to resist a third, a navy blue polka dot.

Feeling profligate, she watched as the most senior of the saleswomen totalled up a very long column of figures. The assistant, though, seemed to find nothing unusual in this astounding spending spree and, smiling at Nancy, promised that her purchases would be packed and delivered to Cavendish Street that afternoon. And that was it. No price tags—the saleswomen had been careful to keep them out of Nancy's sight—no bills, no money passing hands. It was as though such things didn't exist. How extraordinary to live like this.

An hour or so of trying on clothes had been thirsty work and, discovering a ten-shilling note in her purse, Nancy set out to find the store café. Fortified there by sandwiches and a pot of tea, she was ready to tackle the next job on her list: the hairdresser. At the salon her hair was shampooed, her head massaged, and her long waves skilfully cut into a shoulder-length bob. Clamped beneath the hood of a hairdryer, she had time to think at last.

Her thoughts were not exactly cheerful. Leo had been cock-a-hoop at breakfast this morning. He hadn't stopped smiling since she'd agreed to marry, hadn't stopped reminding her of how happy she was making him. Nancy was pleased. He deserved happiness. But unease had begun to take hold. Whereas yesterday she'd allowed herself to think the road of least resistance was the best she could take, today that road looked strewn with obstacles. She was unsure she had done the right thing for either of them. But what else had been left to her, she argued with herself?

When she returned to Cavendish Street, Leo was lavish in praise of her new hairstyle. 'You look wonderful,' he said. 'You'll knock them dead at the Goring.'

It seemed he had been busy while she'd been sitting under the hairdryer, and had visited the Goring Hotel, which he said was *the* best place to eat, and booked the wedding breakfast.

'It will probably be just the two of us,' he said ruefully. 'I've asked James Conroy to be one of our witnesses—you don't know him, but he's a friend from university days and lives close by in Bayswater. He's off to New York in the evening, though, and won't be able to stay for a meal.'

Leo paused. 'My folks won't be there either.' There was an awkward note in his voice. 'I telephoned home, but Dad and my brother are too tied up with the mine to come to London at such short notice.'

Nancy felt sorry for him. No doubt Leo's family had been less than pleased at his sudden marriage to a woman they'd never met, never even heard of, and a girl years younger than him.

'How about I telephone *your* parents?' Leo asked. 'Maybe it's the right time for you all to start talking.'

Nancy was swift to veto the suggestion. 'No! They mustn't know I've married,' she said firmly. 'They're in touch with Philip and they'd pass on the news. I would feel a great deal safer if he didn't know.'

'Any friends then?'

Nancy shook her head.

'That's sad You'll have no one on your special day.'

'You're wrong. I'll have you, Leo.'

It was a reply that made him smile. And he continued to smile throughout the whole of their wedding day.

After a brief ceremony at the Fitzrovia and congratulations from their two witnesses, one of whom to Nancy's surprise turned out to be Mrs Brindley, they were left alone to take a taxi to the Goring, and a wonderful meal: wedding belle cocktail, a main course of lobster, and a delicate trifle for dessert. And seemingly endless toasts to the beautiful new bride.

Finally, they were back at Cavendish Street and Leo was carrying her over the threshold.

He laughed aloud as he deposited her on the hall carpet. 'Thank goodness you're a lightweight.'

He bent to give her a tender kiss and was about to repeat it when footsteps on the stairs had them both look up. Surely Mrs Brindley had gone home after the ceremony, Nancy thought. But it wasn't Mrs Brindley.

'Archie, old chap, back already! You couldn't have timed it better! I know you've met Nancy before, but today is very different. Come and meet my new wife—Mrs Tremayne.'

Nancy found herself looking into a pair of bright blue eyes. Eyes that were searching, measuring, even hostile. Archie Jago offered his hand and she took it. Something in his touch, though, had her drop the handshake quickly.

'Archie, this is the best day of my life!' Leo exclaimed, his face flushed. 'But tomorrow we've work to do. We leave for Venice in a few days.'

'Sure thing, boss.' His assistant remained unsmiling. 'And will Mrs Tremayne be coming with us?'

'Naturally, she will. Venice will be our honeymoon.'

'But the conference…? '

'The conference sessions won't take up the whole week. I'm sure Nancy can amuse herself while I'm there.'

Archie's face was a studied blank and, in response, Nancy looked directly at him.

'I'm sure I can,' she said, her mouth set firm. And there was a challenge in her voice.

If you've enjoyed this prequel, do please leave a review—a few lines is all it takes and is so helpful to authors and other readers.

And why not follow Nancy to Venice, where she does indeed find something to amuse herself, turning crime fighter and dragging an unwilling Archie into her plans.

*Venetian Vendetta* is out now!

## Other Books by Merryn Allingham

Printed in Great Britain
by Amazon

13934196R00082